Bello:

T0331544

hidden talent rediscovered

Bello is a digital only imprint of Pan Macmillan,
established to breathe new life into previously published,
classic books.

At Bello we believe in the timeless power of the imagination,
of good story, narrative and entertainment and we want to use
digital technology to ensure that many more readers
can enjoy these books into the future.

We publish in ebook and Print on Demand formats
to bring these wonderful books to new audiences.

www.panmacmillan.co.uk/bello

Margaret Pemberton

Margaret Pemberton is the bestselling author of over thirty novels in many different genres, some of which are contemporary in setting and some historical.

She has served as Chairman of the Romantic Novelists' Association and has three times served as a committee member of the Crime Writers' Association. Born in Bradford, she is married to a Londoner, has five children and two dogs and lives in Whitstable, Kent. Apart from writing, her passions are tango, travel, English history and the English countryside.

Margaret Pemberton

AFRICAN ENCHANTMENT

BELL◎

First published in 1982 by Mills and Boon

This edition published 2013 by Bello
an imprint of Pan Macmillan, a division of Macmillan Publishers Limited
Pan Macmillan, 20 New Wharf Road, London N1 9RR
Basingstoke and Oxford
Associated companies throughout the world

www.panmacmillan.co.uk/bello

ISBN 978-1-4472-4477-6 EPUB
ISBN 978-1-4472-4476-9 POD

A CIP catalogue record for this book is available from the British Library.

Visit **www.panmacmillan.com** to read more about all our books
and to buy them. You will also find features, author interviews and
news of any author events, and you can sign up for e-newsletters
so that you're always first to hear about our new releases.

*To Christine Cooper, who would
have gone if she could.*

Chapter One

'Papa! Papa! Please don't die!' Tears streamed down Harriet Latimer's cheeks as she cradled the unconscious figure of her father in her arms. Around her the darkening desert stretched to seeming infinity. Only the palms beneath which they sheltered broke the monotony of the ever-shifting dunes.

Henry Latimer stirred, his eyes fluttering open, glazed and unseeing. 'The Nile,' he muttered, barely coherent. 'The white fountains of the Nile.' Then his breath rasped in his throat and he lay still once more.

She eased his head gently from her lap and covered him with the blanket that was his only protection against the bitter cold of the oncoming night. Fear gripped her, crippling in its intensity. They were nearly a thousand miles south of Cairo, lost in the vast expanse of the Nubian Desert. Her father was dying and her own death could not be more than days away. The oasis they had thought to be their salvation had proved to be waterless; the last of the food had been eaten. Hope, which had sustained them for so long, had finally fled.

A desert gazelle approached the palms, seeking water that did not exist. Harriet's heart began to pound. A gazelle meant meat and meat meant a renewal of hope. Her hands closed around her father's rifle. Swiftly she rose to her feet and took aim. The shot shattered the stillness of the night; the gazelle bounded to safety. The oasis was as deserted as before. The dream of exploration that had burned so brightly lay in dust and ashes. Only death remained.

Raoul Beauvais reined in his horse in a flurry of sand at the sound of the rifle shot. His dark brows met in a deep frown. A rifle was not a tribesman's weapon. With a kick of heel to flank, he wheeled his horse around and galloped hard in the direction of the distant oasis.

The soft sound of hooves penetrated Harriet's distress. She gasped and lowered her hands from her tear-wet cheeks, listening intently. It was no illusion. A horseman was approaching. Hope and fear fought for supremacy. If it was a European, then they were saved. If it was one of the tribesmen who had stolen their camels and provisions, then she faced a more unspeakable death than one from hunger and thirst.

She scrambled to her feet and grasped the stock of the rifle with trembling hands. Behind her, her father lay helpless and silent. Bravely she stood in front of his inert body and lifted the rifle to her shoulder. The white of the flowing Arab robes billowed clearly against the dark horizon. A sob escaped her lips. She would meet with no kindness at such hands. She had no protector. Her only chance of salvation lay in frightening her unwelcome visitor away. Even in the black velvet of night she could see the plumes of sand that flew around him and the lean, powerful lines of his body.

'Halt!' she cried in a trembling voice, her finger tightening around the trigger. 'Halt, or I shoot!'

There was a startled oath and the horse reared as it was sharply reined in.

The stock of the rifle bruised her shoulder, its weight excruciating in her weakened arms.

A deep voice cursed and then the unseen rider continued relentlessly onward.

'*Stop!*' Her voice held panic and fear. With cool insolence the horseman continued to ride towards her. The blood thundered in her ears, her heart hammered wildly. She had no alternative but to shoot. He was in her sights, another few seconds and he would be upon her and it would be too late. With a low moan she closed her eyes and squeezed the trigger.

There came the sound of a body hitting the sand and the terrified whinnying of a horse.

'Oh God!' she sobbed, and opened her eyes. The white-robed body rolled beneath flailing hooves and then sprang upright, sprinting towards her.

Clumsily she tried to reload the rifle and failed. Her hands were shaking, damp with sweat.

'No! *No!*' she cried, as the rifle was seized brutally from her grasp and tossed aside into the darkness.

'You little fool! You nearly killed me!' The voice was tight with anger. 'Where are your companions ... your porters?' The deep, rich voice, speaking English with only the faintest of accents, halted her rising hysteria. She struggled for breath and control.

'Our porters have fled,' she gasped, pressing her hands against her still-racing heart. 'We are alone.' She stepped aside and revealed the unconscious figure of her father.

Raoul moved swiftly, and as he knelt at her father's side, Harriet saw the gleaming curve of a jewelled dagger at his waist. An Arab, he was of a very different breed to the tribesmen who had stolen their camels. Once more hope began to grow tremulously.

'Will you help us?' she asked. 'My father is ill and weak and I must get him to Khartoum as quickly as possible.'

Slowly, Raoul rose to his feet and gazed down at her. She was petite, the gold of her hair scarcely skimming his shoulders. In the brilliantly starred desert night he could see that her face was heart-shaped, her eyes tantalisingly tilted and long-lashed.

He said, with unaccustomed gentleness, 'Khartoum is a long journey from here. You would do better to return to the coast.'

Harriet's veneer of control evaporated. 'We cannot!' Her brave heart nearly failed her at the prospect of retracing her steps across the pitiless desert. 'We have no provisions: tribesmen stole them. We have been wandering, lost and alone, for days ... weeks ... My father will die unless he receives shelter and nourishment ...'

Strong hands reached out for her, grasping her shoulders.

'Your father is already dead,' he said compassionately.

'No,' she whispered, feeling what little strength remained drain out of her body. 'No. Oh no!'

Despairingly she stumbled the few steps to her father's side and sank on to her knees, cradling him in her arms. His dreams of discovery were over. A slight smile remained on his lips as if, at the very end, he had believed them to have been realised.

Raoul watched her silently, grim-faced. His detour was going to cost him several days' travelling time. She would have to be escorted to Khartoum and he would have to remain with her until a suitable escort was found to accompany her back to Cairo. It would be no easy task. Khartoum's inhabitants consisted mainly of Turks and renegades – men who would sell their sisters into slavery if the price were high enough. Uncharitably he cursed the dead man lying a few yards away from him. Whoever he had been, he had been a fool. The Khartoum of the mid eighteen-hundreds was no place for a woman. The most remote city in the world was a pit of iniquity, so far removed from government that it had become a law unto itself, a vast trading post for hapless Africans, bought and sold like cattle. He doubted if the grief-stricken English girl had any idea what lay ahead of her.

She had spoken of Khartoum as if reaching it would end all her troubles. Even his hardened imagination shrank from the thought of what her fate would be in such a city. She could not possibly stay there. Arrangements would have to be made for her to leave immediately: unless he altered direction himself and personally escorted her back to Cairo. He dismissed the idea impatiently. It would take six to eight weeks and it was time he could not spare. Besides, he was not a nursemaid. Her predicament was not of his making.

He said curtly, 'We must be on our way. Travel is easier at night than through the day's heat.'

The harshness of his voice startled her. She turned her head, raising it to his, her eyes pleading.

'Then help me with my father,' she said, her voice thick with suppressed tears as she closed his eyes and pulled the blanket high around him.

'There is no time,' he said, hating himself for his callousness.

Harriet stared at him in bewilderment. 'I do not understand you. It will take only a little while to dig a grave and then . . .'

'I am digging no graves!' The robe that had been covering the lower part of his face fell away as he moved angrily. 'I have been delayed long enough. We leave immediately.'

Harriet stared at him in disbelief. 'You cannot mean to leave him here like that! My father has served his Maker all his life. He deserves a Christian burial.'

Narrowed eyes blazed in a lean, dark face. 'This is the desert. The sand will cover him within hours. Now hurry. I want to be well on my way before sunrise.'

Harriet stared at him aghast. 'You cannot mean it!'

'I assure you I mean every word. Pick up your things.' He gestured towards her discarded hat with its broad brim and veil and the well-worn Bible at her father's side.

'No!' Harriet was trembling, but not with fear. She was trembling with a fury she had never thought herself capable of. She faced the handsome, almost satanic features defiantly. 'You may leave him but I will not! I will bury him myself!'

His eyes blazed and she flinched involuntarily. With an oath he spun on his heel, his robes whipping around his powerful body. For a second she thought he was returning to his horse, but instead he strode to the foot of the nearest palm and began scooping furiously at the sand beneath its shade.

She let out a deep shuddering breath of relief and with her face still wet with tears, walked across the dark, soft sand, kneeling at his side.

The sky was reddening to dawn before their task was complete. It had been accomplished in silence: by Raoul, because to speak would have been to give way to his anger and impatience; by Harriet, because she was numb with grief.

As they leaned back on their heels Raoul said tersely, 'I do not know the order of service for the burial. Will the 23rd Psalm be adequate?'

Harriet brushed the sand from her skirt and rose to her feet, swaying with weariness. 'I do not think that will be suitable,' she said stiffly.

Black brows flew upwards. 'The Lord's Prayer, then?'

She shook her head. 'I do not think it would be proper. You are an Arab and a Muslim . . .'

'I am a Frenchman and a Christian,' he snapped, a dangerous edge to his voice as he opened her father's well-worn Bible.

Half insensible from hunger and exhaustion, Harriet stared at him in disbelief, but did not protest. The well-known words filled the air and then there was no more reason for delay. He strode swiftly towards his horse and she attempted to follow, no longer able to see clearly for the lights that danced before her eyes.

Raoul's face was set in grim, uncompromising lines. In the morning light he had seen that the tilted eyes were golden-green and thickly lashed, the mouth gentle and soft – unknowingly sensual. Staring at her across her father's grave he had wondered what it would be like to kiss and despised himself for his carnality. She was bereaved and alone, helpless in a wilderness barely charted. She needed comfort and he was not accustomed to giving it. She needed escorting and so would delay his own progress. In short, she was a nuisance he could have well done without.

'Please hurry,' he said curtly. 'We have wasted enough time already. If a man wishes to live he does not tarry in the desert.'

She tried to do as he bid, but the palms and the sand, the sky and his fluttering robes, merged into one. With a small cry the darkness closed in on her and she collapsed insensible in the sand.

'What the . . .' He spun round and then broke into a run. Her skin was so pale it was translucent. With dreadful clarity he saw the empty camel bags and realised that she was starving. Cursing himself for a fool he lifted her in his arms and carried her out of the morning sun and into the shade of the palms. She had told him their provisions had been stolen but the significance of her remark had not sunk in. He had assumed that there had been enough to sustain them. Certainly her father had died of heat exhaustion and not lack of food. It was now obvious that his daughter had given him all her rations.

Swiftly he removed a silver flask of brandy from his own pack and biscuits and dates.

As the blood-red mist cleared from her eyes and she regained consciousness, Harriet was aware of strong arms around her and a feeling of safety and refuge. His sun-bronzed face was no longer hard and forbidding. From beneath black brows equally black eyes surveyed her with an expression that was almost considerate.

'When did you last eat?'

She was held close against the warmth of his chest and for some curious reason had no desire to free herself.

'I cannot remember,' she said truthfully.

'Have a mouthful of this. It will revive you.' His arm was around her shoulders, steadying her as she drank from the flask and then choked. A faint smile curved his mouth. 'Hard liquor does not agree with you.'

She tried to regain her composure. 'I am not familiar with it.' She paused, confused as to how to address him.

Raoul screwed the top back on to his flask and handed her biscuits and dates. 'Raoul Beauvais,' he said in reply to her unspoken question. 'I am a naturalist and a geographer.'

She ate the biscuits and dates greedily and saw no reason to remove his arm while she did so. Only when she had eaten the last biscuit did she become aware of the impropriety of their closeness. She tried to pull away but he held her easily.

'You are still too weak to walk,' he said, and ignoring her protest swept her up into his arms and strode with her to where his Arabian stallion waited impatiently.

'Before we travel you need to drink,' he said, setting her once more on her feet as they reached the stallion's side.

She gazed at the hip flask in horror.

'Water,' he said, amusement tinging the hard contours of his mouth as he handed her a leather water bottle. She took it gratefully, the water splashing down and trickling on to her bodice as she drank. The soft swell of her breasts was clearly defined beneath their thin covering, and desire surged through him. He cursed inwardly. After six months of celibacy whilst charting the mountains and rivers of Abyssinia he could have well done without such a companion. It would have been better if she had been an elderly spinster; then the inconvenience of escorting her to safety would not have been compounded by other, baser emotions.

Harriet handed back the water flask, overcome with sudden shyness. He looked more like an Arab prince than a European. His hair was thick and black, glossy as a raven's wing. His skin was olive-toned, his eyes dark and unfathomable. The strong, hawk-like face both attracted and disturbed her. He was like no man she had ever met before. He offered her no word of comfort, barely any kindness, yet there was something sensitive as well as sensual in the lines of his well-shaped mouth. His masculinity overpowered her. He moved swiftly and purposefully and with utter self-assurance. A little pulse began to beat wildly in her throat as he swung agilely into his saddle and then lifted her bodily in front of him.

As his hands circled her waist something hot flickered at the back of his eyes to be immediately suppressed. 'We have a long journey ahead of us – and an uncomfortable one. I trust you are not a complaining female.'

'I have never been accused of it!' Harriet said, stung to anger.

His eyes gleamed in the darkness. 'You still have not told me your name.'

'Miss Latimer,' Harriet said tightly, aware that she was being held in an improperly close embrace. 'Harriet Latimer.'

'And what, Miss Latimer, were you and your father doing trying to cross the Nubian Desert without porters or provisions?'

'Our porters fled and our provisions were stolen,' Harriet said simply.

He frowned. 'But you have not told me why you were journeying southwards into an uncharted wilderness.'

Harriet's chin tilted defiantly upward. 'It was our intention to discover the source of the Nile.'

He laughed mirthlessly. 'If explorers like Richard Burton and John Speke failed to find the Nile's source, an elderly man and a mere girl could not possibly do so. Your expedition was one conceived by a fool.'

Harriet swung to face him and raised her hand to deliver a stinging blow to his cheek. 'How dare you speak of my father so!'

He seized her wrist in a steel-like grip. 'Because it's true,' he said, eyes flashing. 'No one but a fool would set out for Khartoum with such a small party. As for travelling further into regions still unmapped . . . Only a madman would consider it.'

'My father was neither mad nor a fool.' Her voice shook with fury. 'He was a missionary who was fully aware of the dangers he faced.'

Raoul's face was grim. 'He was a fool,' he reiterated. 'A man who knew of the dangers would never have brought his child with him.'

'I am not a child!' Angry colour flooded her cheeks. 'I am eighteen and as able to face danger as any man!'

'I can hardly imagine having to carry a man in my arms,' Raoul said drily.

Harriet choked with impotent rage and did not deign to reply to him. She had been saved but the cost was great; enforced company with a man who did not even have the semblance of good manners. A man insolent, insulting and devastatingly handsome.

The last thought had come unbidden. She dug her nails deep into her palms, acutely conscious that the cantering of the horse obliged her to be in almost constant bodily contact with him.

'Who do you know in Khartoum who will be able to escort you the fifteen-hundred miles back to Cairo?' he asked, breaking the hostile silence that had fallen between them.

'No one.'

His frown deepened. 'It will take months for word of your plight to reach England and your mother.'

She kept her back firmly turned against him, surveying the dunes with bleak eyes. 'I have no mother. She died when I was three.'

'But you have family?' A note of alarm had crept into his voice.

'I have two maiden aunts. Both of them are over eighty. I have no intention of returning to them.'

'You have no option.'

She swung round again and met his eyes defiantly. 'I lived with them in Cheltenham after my mother's death until the beginning

9

of this year. I shall not live with them again. My parents were missionaries in Cairo. I was born in Africa. I shall remain in Africa.'

Tiny green sparks flashed in her eyes. Raoul clenched his jaw. Miss Harriet Latimer was going to be even more trouble than he had originally envisaged.

'You can stay in Cairo and rot in Cairo for all I care,' he said cruelly. 'But Cairo is not Khartoum.'

'In what way does it differ, Mr Beauvais?' Harriet asked tartly.

Raoul thought of the slave traders and had an overpowering urge to shake her by the shoulders. 'Khartoum is the last refuge of the scum of Europe,' he said brusquely. 'It is a city outside the law, a city inhabited by murderers and worse.'

'And is it a city that is your own destination?' Harriet asked silkily.

Raoul fought down his rising anger. She was goading him on purpose and he would not give her the satisfaction of allowing her to see that the barb had struck home.

'Yes,' he replied shortly and dug his heels into the stallion's side, urging it to a gallop.

Harriet gasped and fell back with her full weight against him as they streaked over the dunes. Dignity was impossible. She wound her fingers into the stallion's mane and struggled to stay upright.

'It would be easier if you rested your weight against my chest.'

'Never!'

He shrugged indifferently. 'If you fall you have no one to blame but yourself.'

'I shall not fall, Mr Beauvais,' she hissed, her body aching with the effort to remain upright.

'I trust you are not going to be so maidenly when it comes to sharing the same tent, Miss Latimer.'

Harriet choked. 'I may be forced to travel in this undignified manner with you, Mr Beauvais, but nothing on God's earth would persuade me to share a tent with you!'

'That is a relief, Miss Latimer. The tent is small and I would have been greatly inconvenienced.'

'Then rest easy,' she spat through clenched teeth. 'I shall not be inconveniencing you. Now or ever!'

The morning sun was rising high in the sky. The heat was stunning. Sand stretched undulatingly as far as the eye could see. Sand and a searing blue sky and occasionally a cluster of sun-bleached rocks.

Against her will her eyes began to close and there was a suspicion of a smile on Raoul's hard mouth as she gradually leant with increasing ease and unconsciousness against his chest.

When she awoke it was midday and the light was blinding. She blinked, momentarily disorientated, expecting to see the familiarity of a little rosewood dressing table and the water colours that hung on her bedroom wall. Instead there was a handful of palms and endless sand and she was leaning with undue familiarity against a Frenchman in flowing Arab robes. She removed herself from the comfort of the crook of his arm and said,

'I had fallen asleep. It will not happen again.'

He slipped from the saddle and said with lazy insolence, 'It is of no moment. I have carried sick natives thus on far longer journeys.'

She glared at him venomously but he seemed totally unconcerned at her fury and even had the temerity to circle her waist with his hands and lift her to the ground. She pushed away from him, her skirts swishing. Raoul slid his saddlebags over his shoulder and strode to the nearest palm, sitting in its shade. White rocks and scrub surrounded the meagre oasis and Harriet sat on a scorching boulder and fumed. One day's travel had brought them to another oasis. It would have done so if she and her father had been able to continue. By now, if her father had been stronger, they would have been safely on their way to Khartoum. Instead she was forced to endure the company of a man who made free with her with presumptuous carelessness. The water bottle was at his side and he was eating a leisurely breakfast of biscuits and dates. The rock she was sitting on was unbearably hot. She was thirsty and tired and her limbs ached from the ceaseless movement of the horse.

Raoul sighed. She was stubborn enough to remain in the heat of the sun all day unless he coaxed her into a better temper. His fingertips had met as they circled her waist. It had been a long time since he had enjoyed such a pleasant experience. He said, with unaccustomed patience, 'You will need to drink and eat. Otherwise you will have no strength to continue the journey.'

Harriet fought an inward battle. She wanted nothing to do with Mr Beauvais. Yet common sense told her she could not remain in the glare of the sun, sulking, without food and water for ever.

Reluctantly she moved forward, sitting a suitable distance away from him, accepting the biscuits and dates and the water bottle with chilling politeness. As she ate he erected the tent in what shade he could find. A Persian carpet was unrolled and laid inside. Harriet's tired limbs ached for the comfort of lying on it. She watched him covertly as he tended to his horse. There was an unleashed power about his movements that reminded her of the grace and deadliness of a powerful animal. In the morning light his black hair had taken on a blue sheen and his lean face, with its firm jaw and finely chiselled mouth, looked more foreign than ever. She averted her head quickly as he turned towards her, saying, 'Have you reconsidered your decision to rest in the open?'

'There is as much shade here as I have enjoyed these last few weeks.'

Though she could not see it, there was grudging admiration in his eyes. 'Maybe, but you had reservoirs of strength to draw on then. Now you have none. I suggest that you rest as comfortably as possible.'

Harriet eyed the cool opening to the tent longingly.

'It will only be for a few hours. Rest in the desert is of necessity minimal.'

'Then I will rest,' she said stiffly, despising herself for the weakness of her body.

His mouth curved into a smile and for a brief moment he looked almost approachable as she crossed to the tent and entered the welcome shade. Gratefully she undid the high-necked fasteners of her blouse in order to breathe more freely and removed the high-buttoned boots which had seemed so sensible in Cheltenham and which had proved so uncomfortable in the desert. In utter weariness she stretched herself on the luxury of the Persian carpet and closed her eyes. They opened almost immediately as a dark shadow fell across her.

'How dare you, Sir!' She sat up instantly, oblivious that the buttons of her blouse were undone revealing the creamy whiteness of her breasts.

Raoul shrugged. 'I told you that such a small tent would be inconveniencing.'

Harriet scrambled to her knees. 'You didn't tell me that you would be sharing it with me!'

'An oversight. I thought the position was perfectly clear. I have ridden hard and require sleep. At great discomfort to myself I am prepared to share my sleeping quarters.'

'I, Mr Beauvais, am not prepared to share them with you!'

He held back the flap of the tent and said smoothly, 'Then leave, Miss Latimer. I wouldn't dream of detaining you by force.'

Outside the sun seared the rocks and sand with merciless heat. Harriet felt tears of frustration and anger well in her eyes as she accepted defeat. Raoul Beauvais' insufferable nearness was preferable to the discomfort that awaited her outside the shelter of the tent. Mutely she lay down once again, turning her back towards him, every line of her body signifying her outrage.

There came the sound of his dagger being unbuckled and laid aside. Her cheeks burned: surely he was not going to disrobe? Her heart beat shallow and fast. And then she heard him lying down and knew that if she moved by as much as an inch she would be in bodily contact with him. She closed her eyes, praying for sleep and an escape from her mortification. Not for a long time were her prayers answered.

When she awoke it was still light but she was alone. From outside came the sound of the horse moving listlessly and saddlebags being flung over its back. She rose hastily and emerged into the sunlight, blinking. Raoul turned to her.

'I trust you slept well, Miss Latimer, despite the unwelcome company.'

She did not reply and his eyes gleamed in his sun-bronzed face.

'Perhaps you would like the use of a hairbrush, Miss Latimer. You are beginning to look a little . . . dishevelled.'

His eyes slid with open admiration down to her breasts. With a gasp she clasped her blouse together and swung round, fastening her buttons with trembling fingers, her face scarlet. How long had she lain exposed to his gaze in the intimacy of the tent? How many more humiliations would she have to suffer before their journey was over?

'I am ready to leave, Miss Latimer.' The tent was speedily dismantled and rolled into a pack. He was already astride his horse. She had no way of mounting apart from accepting his proffered hand as he leant down and swung her up in front of him. Rested and refreshed she was more acutely aware than ever of his uncomfortable nearness – and her predicament. She knew no one in Khartoum. She was without family and without friends. Except, perhaps, for the British Consul.

'Do you know Lord Crale, the British Consul in Khartoum?' she asked hesitantly. 'I believe my father informed him of our expected arrival.'

'Let's hope so,' Raoul said grimly. 'At least there you will be given shelter.'

Her optimism, temporarily quenched, returned. 'Then I have no problem.'

'You have every problem. You cannot stay in Khartoum. I have already told you what kind of a city it is. You will have to journey back across the Nubian Desert and then voyage once more down the Nile to Cairo. It is a journey that would make a man flinch.'

Her optimism had overcome her anger. Her eyes sparkled as she said spiritedly, 'But I am not a man, Mr Beauvais.'

Raoul clenched his jaw. He was becoming more aware of that with every passing second.

'You are as empty-headed as all your sex,' he said through clenched teeth.

Harriet laughed, determined that nothing should destroy her good humour now that she had regained it. 'Why, Mr Beauvais, I do believe you are a woman hater.'

Despite himself Raoul found the corner of his mouth lifting in amusement. He had been labelled many things in his thirty-two years, but never that.

Thorn scrub and yellow rock began to break up the monotony of the blinding dunes. Harriet gestured towards them.

'Does that mean we are nearing Khartoum?'

'It means we are approaching the Nile again. The journey to Khartoum will still take several weeks but it will not be so arduous. We shall soon be able to travel by dhow.'

Harriet's spirits soared. She had travelled the Nile by dhow with her father as far as Korosko and had enjoyed the experience immensely. At Korosko the Nile deviated from its course south in a gigantic, cataract-filled loop that could not be sailed. It was then that they had had to resort to camels to cross the desert to the point where the Nile once again flowed south towards Khartoum.

Raoul Beauvais' eyes rested on her with disquieting frequency. He had never before been attracted to an English girl. Their manner was too stiff, their beauty too chill, more like that of marble statues than flesh-and-blood women. However, the one in his arms was a far cry from those he had met on the boring social rounds of Cairo and Alexandria. She had both spirit and courage. To have crossed the Nubian desert with no companion other than a sick father was no mean feat. He remembered the way she had faced him with a rifle and was grateful that she was unfamiliar with the weapon. The shot she had fired had come disconcertingly close. She shifted in her sleep and he slipped his arm more comfortably around her. Her hair, so neatly coiled throughout the day, was becoming dishevelled, the pins loosening. He wondered how long it was and touched it lightly. It was silky soft, the colour of early wheat. The long lashes that fanned her cheeks were golden tipped and lustrous. Miss Harriet Latimer was extraordinarily beautiful. He took comfort in the fact. Her presence was an inconvenience but one that was becoming increasingly pleasant.

The shrubs thickened and became greener. Raoul breathed a sigh of relief. Once they reached the banks of the Nile their journey would be relatively easy. Even for a traveller as experienced as himself, the desert was always full of unknown dangers.

When Harriet opened her eyes again darkness had fallen. She was held securely in Raoul Beauvais' arms. She wondered how he managed to hold her for so long without being overcome by tiredness, and then her eyes closed and she fell once more into exhausted sleep. The movement of the horse and the cold woke her intermittently. Once or twice she looked up at the face only inches from her own and studied the abrasive masculine lines of nose and mouth. Drowsy with slumber, she remained close to him, the warmth from his body spreading through her.

'The Nile,' Raoul announced, hours later, rousing her.

It was dawn and the scrub had merged into verdant green bushes and shrubs. The river flowed murky and milky coloured; a broad, mile-wide expanse that cried out to be bathed in.

'Thank goodness!' she cried, her face elated as he swung her to the ground. Unhesitatingly she ran to its banks and bent down, letting the water trickle through her fingers, saying in mock annoyance, 'Why can't it flow in a straight line and make life easier for people, instead of meandering for hundreds of miles in a loop that is of no use to anyone?'

'Nature is extremely unbiddable,' Raoul said drily.

Harriet laughed. 'And uncomfortable. I shall probably stay in Khartoum for the rest of my life rather than face that hateful desert again.'

Raoul did not reply. With the swift, spare movements that she was becoming accustomed to, he erected the tent and unrolled the Persian carpet. She sat down on it thankfully. Every bone in her body ached with the discomfort of the journey.

'Here are the dates and biscuits,' he said, handing her the saddlebags. 'I'm going to try and shoot some pigeon or quail. We both of us need a hot meal. I have had a surfeit of dates!'

Harriet hadn't. She ate them gratefully while he removed a rifle from his pack.

Their previous rest had been short, only a few hours at the most. She wondered how he managed on so little sleep and watched him as he strode away, the rifle over his shoulder. She was alone in the hot silence. Her blouse was clinging to her. Her skirt was encrusted with dust and sand. If she washed them in the river they would soon dry and she could bathe herself, removing the grime of countless days. With unspeakable relief she removed her buttoned boots and wiggled her toes freely. She could sleep in her camisole and underskirt, modestly covered by Raoul Beauvais' blanket, while her garments dried. The sand was excruciatingly hot beneath her bare feet. Picking up her skirts, she ran down to the bank and shivered with delight as she stepped into the cool water. She looked around but there was no sign of Raoul Beauvais.

Quickly she divested herself of her blouse and skirt and stepped further from the bank and rushes, letting the water slide up and over her legs until it reached her waist. Then she plunged her blouse and skirt into the water and began to rub vigorously. From somewhere amongst the reeds a bird sang and she hummed along with it. The sight of the Nile had restored her spirits. It was a sight she had thought she would never live to see again. She wrung her garments out and threw them on to the bank and then she shook the remaining pins from her hair. It hung, waist-length, rippling down over her lace-trimmed camisole and trailing in the water. With a little gasp of pleasure she moved deeper, luxuriating in the feel of the water against her sweat-soaked skin. A volley of rifle shots rang out and she wondered if Raoul had been successful in his venture. She let the water take her weight, her hair fanning out in the current. Never before had she realised the unspeakable luxury of bathing.

'I would ask you to return to the bank before you are joined by hungry crocodiles,' a familiar voice said lazily.

Harriet gasped and forgot her efforts to float. He was sitting on a rock, two birds slung over his shoulder, his rifle in his hand.

'Crocodiles!' Eyes wide with horror she clumsily waded to the bank and so great was her distress that not until she had clambered out amongst the reeds and rushes, did she realise that she was minus her blouse and skirt.

'Perhaps next time you wish to bathe, you will tell me and I will stand guard.' He was eying her with unconcealed admiration, his eyes bold and black and frankly appraising.

'You are impertinent, Mr Beauvais!' It was difficult to climb through the reeds with any semblance of dignity. Her lawn camisole and underskirt clung to her as if they were invisible.

'You are ravishing, Miss Latimer,' he said sincerely.

With a final effort she freed herself from the last of the reeds and slapped him across the face with all the strength she possessed. He caught her easily, holding her fast, his mouth coming down on hers in swift, unfumbled contact. She struggled but to no avail. It was her first kiss and one that was given with expert thoroughness. Not until she had stopped struggling did Raoul release her. When he did, his robe was damp where her breasts had been pressed close to his chest and there was an unreadable expression in the back of his eyes.

'There are birds to cook,' he said tersely, and leaving her gasping for breath and composure, he pivoted on his heels and strode away towards the camp.

Chapter Two

Harriet pushed wet tendrils of hair away from her face with a trembling hand, her whole body shaking with rage and indignation. He had taken advantage of her. He had ... Vainly she sought for a suitable word. He had *violated* her. He was no gentleman; no suitable companion to travel alone with across miles of uncharted desert. She pressed her hands against her burning cheeks, still feeling the hot imprint of his lips on hers. His behaviour had been unspeakable. Half falling, she sank on to a sun-scorched rock. He had kissed her until her senses had reeled and had not cared if she had been willing or not. Her cheeks burned more hotly than ever. Had she been totally unwilling? In those last, final moments when his mouth had seared hers with his strong arms holding her fast, had she not submitted, her lips parting helplessly beneath his?

Shame engulfed her. Had he known? Had he been triumphant as he strode away? She remembered the taut lines of his body, the enigmatic expression in the near-black of his eyes. No, there had been no triumph there. Anger seeped through her, overcoming shame. He had been indifferent, thinking only of the birds he had shot that needed roasting. The kiss he had forced from her had been meaningless to him. Her eyes sparkled with fury. The rock was uncomfortably hot, the sand unbearable beneath her naked feet. She could not remain at the river bank for ever. Behind her she could hear the sound of fire crackling and despite herself her mouth watered. It had been weeks since she had eaten anything but meagre rations. Sooner or later the insufferable Mr Beauvais would have to be faced. Her blouse and skirt were still wet. She had nothing with which to cover herself. Despairingly she pulled on the wet clothes and, tossing her hair over her shoulders, walked defiantly towards the tent and the small campfire. He was squatting Indian fashion on his heels, turning a makeshift spit above the fire, the smell of roast meat filling the air. At her appearance he raised his head, his eyebrows raising fractionally at the sight of her in the dripping garments.

'The sun would have dried them within minutes.'

'I have no desire to remain unclothed for even a short space of time,' Harriet snapped.

His mouth tightened. 'Your virtue is quite safe, Miss Latimer.'

'It did not seem so a minute ago!'

He shrugged. 'A mere kiss. Surely you've been kissed before, Miss Latimer.'

His white shirt was open to the waist, revealing whipcord muscles and an indecent amount of dark, curly hair. She averted her gaze, saying stiffly, 'I find your question as impertinent as your behaviour, Mr Beauvais.'

'My apologies, Miss Latimer. I had not realised that you were scarce out of the schoolroom. Rest assured I will treat you . . . parentally . . . until we reach Khartoum.'

Harriet stamped her feet, her hair falling in wild disarray over her shoulders, 'I am *not* a child, Mr Beauvais. Before I came to Egypt I had already turned down several proposals of marriage!'

'Several?' Satanic brows flew upwards.

Harriet had not been brought up to lie. She struggled inwardly for a moment and then said defiantly, 'One gentleman in particular was most desirous that I should become his wife.'

With difficulty Raoul kept the laughter from his voice. 'And in what way did the gentleman prove lacking, Miss Latimer?'

Harriet thought of her suitor, the Reverend March-Allinson, of his wispy hair and his fumbling ineptness.

'I have no desire for marriage, Mr Beauvais.'

'Very commendable, Miss Latimer. Neither have I.'

Across the flames their eyes met. Harriet's furiously angry, Raoul Beauvais' strangely challenging.

'Then I have your promise that there will be no repeat of . . . of . . .'

'. . . my disgraceful behaviour?' he finished for her easily. 'None at all. It was a mere whim, Miss Latimer. Nothing more.'

Her palm itched to slap his face and she felt an overwhelming desire to drum her booted feet into his shins with all the force she possessed. She could not even flounce away in anger for if she did so he would eat the pigeon alone and she ached with hunger. Instead she sat primly on the far side of the fire, her arms hugging her knees, her still-damp skirt and blouse clinging to her uncomfortably. She had not rebraided her hair and it hung in a shiny mass across her shoulders and down her back, the last golden curl reaching the base of her spine. Raoul removed the pigeon from the spit and skewered on another, doubting if any man before him had had the pleasure of seeing Miss Harriet Latimer so deliciously disarrayed. He had been glad of her delay at the river bank. It had given him time to get his own emotions well under control. He had been a fool to have kissed her, genteel young ladies were apt to read into such an embrace far more than it held. At thirty-two he was a free man and intended to stay that way. Accompanying her alone to Khartoum was going to cause raised eyebrows and no doubt some foolish busybody would put the idea into Miss Latimer's golden head that after having her reputation so seriously tarnished, the only recompense was marriage, especially when that marriage would be to the eldest son of one of the wealthiest families in France.

His fears had proved groundless. Harriet Latimer was not the husband-hunter that the majority of her sex were. The indignation had been real, as had her avowal that she had no desire for marriage, which was for some man, somewhere, a pity. Miss Harriet Latimer was definitely not destined to become an old maid. He remembered the pressure of her small, high breasts against his chest; the pleasurable smallness of her waist and the soft, vulnerability of her lips. There had been a brief moment when her clenched fists had ceased pounding his shoulders and her mouth had parted willingly. The prim and proper Miss Harriet Latimer had been on

21

the verge of answering passion with passion. It was that knowledge that had brought him to his senses. He wanted no clinging female in his life – only freedom.

He handed her the roast meat and she took it in her fingers. He watched her with interest. Nothing in Harriet's background could have prepared her for the ordeal she was now undergoing. She was a missionary's daughter, brought up by maiden aunts; her whole eighteen years spent in sheltered, cloistered surroundings. Yet here she was, eating with her fingers, ignoring discomfort that would make hardened soldiers quail and looking almost paganly beautiful with her streaming, sun-gold hair.

She licked her fingers clean, drank deeply from the water bottle and then regarded the shadowed entrance of the tent with troubled eyes.

He knew what she was thinking and remained silent, watching her as he ate. Harriet took a deep breath and said with an underlying tremble in her voice, 'After the unfortunate incident in the river, Mr Beauvais, I am sure you will agree that it is impossible for us to share the same sleeping accommodation.'

Raoul broke off a piece of meat from a bone and said lazily, 'Would you prefer me to place your blanket immediately outside the tent, or would that be too intimate? Perhaps it would be better some distance away. By the banks of the river, though of course there are the crocodiles to take into consideration.'

Harriet sprang to her feet, almost sobbing with frustration. 'You know perfectly well what I mean, Mr Beauvais. It is *you*, not I, who must sleep elsewhere!'

'But it is my tent,' he pointed out with infuriating politeness.

Harriet stamped her foot in the sand. '*You* are *supposed* to be a gentleman!'

He smiled, a slow, devastating smile that sent the colour rushing to her cheeks. 'But we both know that that isn't so, don't we, Miss Latimer?'

His voice was caressing and there was a wicked gleam in his eyes as he rose to his feet.

Hastily she backed away. 'You gave me your word that you would not lay a hand on me again!'

He paused and said regretfully, 'So I did. A shame when there is so little else to divert us.'

'Mr Beauvais,' Harriet said chokingly, 'will you please stop making amusement of my predicament.'

The laughter faded from his eyes. He threw the last of the pigeon bones to one side and said formally, 'My apologies. The tent is yours, Miss Latimer. We shall continue travelling at dusk.'

Swiftly he removed a blanket from the tent and strode to the nearest sand dune. There was no shade, no palms, no boulders. Hesitantly Harriet walked across to the tent. The Persian carpet was unrolled. Biscuits, dates and the water bottle thoughtfully provided. With a strange heaviness of spirit she removed her boots and lay down. The morning sun was rising rapidly, burning and scorching, unbearable in its intensity. She closed her eyes and tried to sleep, and could not. He would not survive a day exposed without shade. He would die, if not immediately, then the next day or the day after, and she would be his murderer. She opened her eyes and tried to settle herself more comfortably.

Even in the shade of the tent the heat was overwhelming. She opened the buttons of her blouse and wiped the beads of sweat from her forehead. He had given his word that he would not touch her again. For the sake of propriety she was insisting that he suffer the tortures of the sun. If he was not a gentleman, he would not do so. His very action in removing himself showed that he had some moral sense. She crept to the entrance of the tent and peeped out. He appeared to be sleeping, the folds of the head-dress pulled across his face. She bit her bottom lip thoughtfully. If he promised not to take liberties with her person, then surely it would be only Christian to allow him to share the shade of the tent with her.

With her heart throbbing uncomfortably fast she stepped out into the glaring heat and ran lightly across to where he lay. Gently she touched him on the arm.

'Mr Beauvais, Mr Beauvais?'

There was no movement. A small knot of apprehension began

to form in the pit of her stomach. Surely he could not have fallen asleep so quickly. Perhaps already he was suffering from heat stroke.

'Mr Beauvais,' she said urgently, shaking his shoulders.

Again there was no movement.

With a stifled sob she reached across him and felt for his wrist and pulse. Immediately her hand was seized and imprisoned, the robes falling from his face, his eyes so close to hers that she could see tiny flecks of gold near the pupils.

'Let me go!' She wrenched her hand from his grasp and he let it go so suddenly that she fell backwards in the sand.

'I thought you were a hostile Arab,' he said, white teeth flashing as she struggled to her feet, brushing the sand from her skirt and pushing her hair away from her eyes.

'Liar! You knew very well it was me.'

'True,' he agreed, rising easily to his feet. 'Arabs do not smell so sweetly.'

'Don't you wish to know my reason for disturbing you?' Harriet asked, feeling a ridiculous rush of pleasure at his observation.

'No.' Already he was striding confidently towards the tent. 'I know the reason.' He paused at the entrance and held the flap back for her. 'Christian conscience. How could a missionary's daughter allow a man to die within yards of her, unaided and helpless?'

'You're laughing at me!' Harriet said through clenched teeth.

His smile widened. 'Against my will, I find you give me great pleasure, Miss Latimer.'

She stepped into the shade, seething, already regretting her decision. Instead of being grateful he was being impudent. It would have served him right if her Christian conscience had lain dormant.

'I find you insufferable, Mr Beauvais,' she said tightly as she lay down, rolling herself as far as possible away from him. He unclasped the jewelled dagger at his waist and stretched himself comfortably at her side.

'I find you enchanting, Miss Latimer,' he said, and within minutes his breathing was the deep, rhythmical sound of sleep.

Sleep did not come so easily to Harriet. Her emotions were in tumult. She looked across at him; at the winged eyebrows and long, dark lashes. At the strong, aquiline nose and high cheekbones that gave his face such a compelling appearance; at the sensual mouth. A heat that did not come from the sun suffused her body at the memories his mouth evoked. That incident was best forgotten.

He had removed his head-dress to sleep and black curls tumbled low over his brow. It was hair a woman would envy; thick and glossy, springy as heather. She resisted the urge to touch it and as the sun reached its midday crescendo, wondered who this man was who slept at her side. He knew all about her, yet she knew only that his name was Raoul Beauvais and that he was a geographer. What had brought him to Africa in the first place? What kept him here? From the deep olive tones of his skin he had lived and worked in the country for many years. Surely a geographer would be part of an organised expedition – one that would last several months, one year or two at the most. Why was he travelling alone? Where were his companions? And then there was his fluent English. He spoke it colloquially and with only the merest hint of an accent. Had he lived in England, and if so, when and where? What were his plans when he had reached Khartoum? Where next would he map and chart?

She sighed and hugged her knees. Wherever it was, she would not be with him. She would be in Khartoum and then once again she would have to face the arduous journey back to Cairo and the long boat trip home. She sighed again and lay down. All her father's dreams had been in vain. Silent tears of grief slid down her face as she closed her eyes and slept.

Her sleep was disturbed and uneasy. In the late afternoon Raoul rose and gazed at her with a deep frown as she tossed and turned, calling out inarticulately. Her hair was a tumbled mass, her breasts heaving beneath their light covering, the opened buttons exposing more than was respectable to his gaze.

He crossed to her, kneeling at her side, shaking her shoulders gently to rouse her.

Her eyes flew open, wide and unseeing. 'Papa! Papa!' she cried tormentedly.

She was cradled against a strange chest, a deep rich voice said soothingly, 'Hush now, you have had a bad dream.' He was rocking her gently against him as once, many years ago, her father had rocked her when she was a child. The dream fled and reality overwhelmed her. She clung to him, sobbing violently.

'It was not a bad dream!' she gasped at last. 'It was the truth! Papa is dead!'

'Cry,' he said with unaccustomed gentleness. 'Cry until you can cry no more,' and as the sky slowly reddened he held her in his arms and she gave vent to her grief unrestrainedly.

It was dark by the time her harsh sobs had subsided. She lay, spent and exhausted. He stroked her hair, letting it slide through his fingers, marvelling at its silky texture.

He was wearing the shirt and breeches he wore beneath his flowing robes. The heat of his body was comforting. She felt curiously safe and secure. When at last she could speak she said awkwardly,

'I am afraid I have ruined your shirt, Mr Beauvais.'

Raoul gazed down at the lace-edged linen that had been used as a handkerchief and said, 'It is of no matter. You needed to cry. Grief cannot be carried inwardly.'

She moved away from him stiffly, aware that his shirt was undone and that her tear-wet cheeks had been pressed close against the nakedness of his chest.

'You must think me very weak for crying so.'

'On the contrary, I think you very brave.'

At the tone of his voice she raised startled eyes to his. The hard lines of his mouth had softened. There was an expression in his eyes she had never seen before.

'Mr Beauvais . . .' she began hesitatingly, and then she was silenced as he lowered his head and his mouth claimed hers, warm and demanding. This time she did not struggle. She could not. She yielded utterly, her arms circling his neck, her body melting shamelessly against his.

It was her passionate response that brought him to his senses. Miss Harriet Latimer was not a lady of dubious reputation. She was young and innocent and would expect lovemaking to be

26

accompanied by avowals of lifelong devotion and a wedding ring. He released her abruptly. He had no intention of allowing himself to be compromised in such a way. Marriage was for fools.

He said smoothly, 'It is already dark. We must leave immediately if we are to make good time through the night.'

Disentangling himself from her embrace, he swirled his Arab robes over his shirt and tightly trousered and booted legs and strode away. Bewilderedly Harriet followed him. What had happened? Why was he suddenly so indifferent? Carpet and blankets were rolled expertly. The tent was dismantled and packed. Dazedly Harriet stood and watched him, waiting for a glance, a word. Anything that would reassure her that his tenderness had not been a figment of her imagination.

He saw her perplexity and hated himself for the momentary weakness that had caused it.

He said a little less curtly, 'Here is a hairbrush. Your hair will fly in my face unless it is braided.'

Obediently she took the proffered hairbrush and began to smooth her hair with long, rhythmic strokes, coiling it and fastening it in the nape of her neck.

Raoul breathed a sigh of relief. He had bedded females of many nationalities but had never before met one with such astonishing hair. It would have filled an angel from heaven with lust, let alone a full-blooded Frenchman.

He vaulted into the saddle and stretched down his hands to lift her in front of him. She hesitated for a moment.

'Have I behaved ... in an unseemly manner?' she asked uncertainly, her hair shining in the early evening dusk like an angelic halo.

He sighed and swung her up in front of him. 'It is I who have behaved unseemingly, Harriet. Your position is delicate enough without my making matters worse. If I am to escort you as far as Khartoum, then it will have to be without any further such incidents.'

The horse began to canter forward in the darkness and Harriet felt a measure of reassurance. It was the first time he had used her first name and he had done so easily and warmly. She understood what he was saying to her, and knew he was right. He was protecting her reputation. It would suffer enough damage when they reached Khartoum and it became known that they had travelled without even a servant as chaperon. Once she was installed beneath the Consul's roof, Raoul would be able to pay court to her quite openly.

Through the long night hours she thought of her father, but this time without pain. Africa had been his home. She had known the minute she had set foot on Egyptian soil that it would be hers. Innocently she closed her eyes and dreamed of a life that contained both the country of her birth, and the enigmatic Frenchman who had saved her life.

Raoul let out an imperceptible sigh of relief. He had not wanted to hurt her; nor had he wanted to have an hysterical female on his hands. Harriet had not let him down. She had accepted his apology for the kiss in a manner that was extraordinary in a woman. He was not accustomed to meeting beautiful women who also had the benefit of sense. From now on he would utterly forbid her to unpin her hair and he would keep a tight rein on his desires. Once at Khartoum his duty would be discharged and he could seek his pleasure elsewhere; with native girls who did not expect lovemaking to be accompanied by the bestowal of a wedding ring.

His Arabian stallion took the miles easily, leaving plumes of sand in their wake. Often Harriet raised her head, studying the handsome face with its firm jaw and finely chiselled mouth. A face that was once more undemonstrative and impassive. And would remain so, she reminded herself, until they had reached Khartoum. Held secure in strong arms, she leaned against him the excitement of the unknown once more stirring within her. Her father's death had crushed her spirit of adventure. Now it re-awoke in full measure. Miss Harriet Latimer from Cheltenham would soon be in Khartoum, the most remote city in the world. Even in the darkness she became aware that the vegetation around her was changing. The black outline of rocks and shrubs became more numerous and as the desert dawn came swiftly she gasped with pleasure at the sight of green tabbes-grass and acacias and yellow and red aloes.

'We are here? We have arrived?'

Her innocent pleasure was infectious. Raoul gave one of his rare, down-slanting smiles. 'We are nearly at Berber,' he confirmed.

'Berber? But where is Khartoum?'

Raoul suppressed a surge of annoyance. It seemed that Harriet's unworldly father had told her very little of their route. 'We are still several weeks' travel from Khartoum,' he said with an effort at patience. 'Berber is the only place of consequence before it and I shall be able to procure a horse for you there.'

Harriet sat up straight, looking around her with interest. The sand still stretched limitlessly, but was relieved by scorched, burned, dried-out rocks. There were shrubs and thorn trees and in the distance the graceful sway of desert palms.

'A horseman! Do you see?'

She pointed ahead of them and Raoul nodded. 'It is Hashim.'

'Hashim?' she asked.

'My servant and companion. I should have been in Berber days ago. He has been waiting for me.'

'Oh.' Harriet was slightly nonplussed. It had not occurred to her that anyone would be waiting for him. Nor had it occurred to her that he had an itinerary to keep and that her rescue had perhaps inconvenienced him.

The distant figure galloped joyously to meet them, white teeth flashing in a dark face.

'Effendi! Effendi! I thought you had met with grief!'

'A little,' said Raoul drily, remembering the grave he had left behind him. The horses wheeled close together and he slapped the Arab soundly on the back. The Arab's embrace was more effusive and Harriet found herself crushed between the two of them and taken little note of.

At last the Arab released Raoul's shoulders from a fervent clasp and turned to Harriet, grinning broadly and showing blackened and broken teeth.

'Miss Harriet Latimer,' Raoul said, suppressing a smile as Hashim enthusiastically kissed the backs of Harriet's hands and she strove to hide her distaste.

Hashim's bright black eyes surveyed the slender hands and noted the absence of rings. His master had not then done anything so foolish as to bring a wife back with him from his expedition.

'Miss Latimer was travelling to Khartoum with her father,' Raoul continued. 'Mr Latimer died in the desert and I am therefore escorting Miss Latimer to her destination myself.'

Hashim rolled his eyes to Allah, so that only the whites showed. 'A tragedy,' he said. 'A truly momentous tragedy, effendi.'

Harriet was unaccustomed to servants, yet she felt sure that Hashim was displaying undue familiarity towards Raoul. She glanced swiftly up at him. He was a man who instinctively commanded respect. In repose his face was forbidding. Yet he allowed his servant to greet him as a long-lost brother. Again she wondered about him; his background, his family. It seemed the longer she was in his company the less she knew of him.

Hashim, his welcome over, wheeled his horse around and rode at their side, chattering non-stop to Raoul in Arabic. He was not a young man. His face was lean and leathery, his teeth alarmingly decayed. He wore a loose jacket of white cotton and a *lungi* reaching to sandalled feet. His turban was brilliantly striped and, no doubt, the reason Raoul had recognised him from such a distance. The Arabic flowed between them with ease. Her father had spent a lifetime studying the language and had never mastered it with such fluency. She was so immersed in her thoughts that Raoul's voice startled her when he said,

'What do you think of Berber now that you have arrived?'

She blinked. Ahead of them was a scattering of sun-dried huts and beyond a straggle of mud-brick, single-storey buildings. As they drew nearer she could see that the unmade streets were littered with refuse, starving dogs and pot-bellied children.

'Is this it?' Her face was incredulous, her voice aghast.

He nodded.

'But it's . . . it's *primitive!*'

Raoul stifled a grin; Hashim looked affronted.

'Khartoum is little better.'

Harriet gazed around her, unusually silent. The heat and the smells were overpowering. She felt suddenly sick. Khartoum *had* to be better than Berber. It *had* to be.

The huts were by-passed. For a second Harriet thought they were leaving Berber as rapidly as they had entered. Tired and exhausted though she was, she felt only relief. It seemed impossible that Berber could offer any suitable accommodation.

'Will we stay long at the Pasha's?' she heard Hashim ask Raoul in English.

'A day. Two at the most. I need a change of horse and must also buy one for Miss Latimer. There are stores to be replenished. We shall need some baggage camels.'

'All is seen to, effendi. I have secured more quinine from the Pasha. Laudanum, camomel, citric acid and julep.'

'And the rest?'

'The brandy, cigars and soaps are already boxed and waiting only for your arrival.'

Soap! The very word made Harriet feel weak with joy. They were approaching a palm-fringed garden. The house beyond, though single-storeyed, was infinitely more substantial than the ones they had passed.

Raoul said thoughtfully, 'This will be your first introduction to local society. For the sake of your reputation, let me make the explanations, Miss Latimer.'

His face was sombre and withdrawn, with no hint of the warmth that had been in it when he had called her Harriet. She looked beyond him to Hashim and thought she understood. Her anxiety lifted. His cool and indifferent manner was for the protection of her reputation.

A flurry of servants surrounded them as they rode in. Harriet was aware that her presence was giving rise to exclamations of curiosity and admiration. Her skirts were fingered and touched repeatedly as Raoul led her through the chattering throng and into the coolness of a courtyard. Fountains splashed soothingly; dark-skinned girls fluttered swiftly out of sight. They were flimsily clothed and veiled, with gold at their wrists and ankles. Harriet stared after them curiously. The servants who had taken their horse and baggage had been poorly dressed. Who, then, were these others? She had no time to ask Raoul. Eager fingers strove to be the first to have the honour of opening the doors on to a lavishly furnished room.

Harriet's eyes, accustomed for so long to only seeing the dazzling monotony of sand and sky, blinked at the plush velvet, the gilt and the gold. However poverty-stricken the outward appearance of Berber, the Pasha lived in sumptuous splendour. He rose to meet them, a big man, his enormous girth emphasised by a scarlet silk cummerbund. His short, stubby fingers were covered in rings, his hair oiled sleekly, his moustaches long and down-curving. Behind him hung the red-crescent flag of the Ottoman Empire.

'Welcome, Capitaine Beauvais.' The cigar was crushed into an onyx ashtray, Raoul's strong hand clasped between soft, flabby ones.

Small black eyes raked Harriet from head to foot with an expression that sent a shiver of distaste down her spine.

'And who is the beautiful lady?' Already her small hand was engulfed in sweaty palms.

'Miss Harriet Latimer,' Raoul replied without expression. 'She was on her way with her father to Khartoum. Sadly, Mr Latimer's health was not strong enough for the conditions in which they were travelling and he died.'

'Ah.' The black eyes sparkled like pinpricks and Harriet was aware of the overpowering smell of cologne. 'So the young lady is without protection?'

'Not so.' Raoul had removed his Arab robes and stood with nonchalant ease in his shirt and breeches, allowing a small, formally dressed negro boy to pour him a large measure of whisky. 'I shall be escorting Miss Latimer to Khartoum.'

Reluctantly Harriet's hand was released. 'I think that would be most unwise, Capitaine. The young lady has just endured terrible hardships. She needs rest and recuperation before continuing south and you, I understand, intend to leave almost immediately.'

Raoul swallowed the whisky and helped himself to more. 'That is correct. My manservant has already seen to the necessary supplies. I shall be leaving as soon as I have procured fresh horses.'

'Then let me suggest,' the Pasha purred, his eyes returning again and again to Harriet's golden hair, 'that Miss Latimer remains here at Berber, until she is rested. It would be a more ... suitable arrangement.'

'I do not think so.'

The Pasha's eyebrows rose in his fleshy face. 'But Capitaine! It would be most unseemly for Miss Latimer to continue to Khartoum accompanied only by yourself and an Arab.'

'Not in the circumstances.' Across the room his eyes held hers. For an earth-shattering moment Harriet thought he was going to declare her his bride-to-be and then he was saying smoothly,

'You see, Miss Latimer and I are cousins.'

'I had not realised the Beauvais family had English connections.' There was rank disbelief in the Pasha's voice.

'Great families have many branches,' Raoul replied smoothly. 'And now I would appreciate it if my cousin could be cared for by your women. She needs to bathe and change. Meanwhile, perhaps we could discuss the purchase of two stallions.'

In vain Harriet tried to catch his eye. She *had* no clothes into which to change. Furthermore, much as she desired a bath, the thought of being led away by an army of women in such a strange and oppressive atmosphere filled her with anxiety. As if intentionally, Raoul kept his eyes averted from her pleading face.

The Pasha clapped his hands imperiously and a score of veiled and bejewelled females entered the room. The Pasha spoke to them silkily in Turkish, but his eyes rested only on Harriet as she was led unwillingly away.

Raoul, well aware of the Pasha's intentions and the spyholes that invaded the privacy of every room, began to talk at tedious length about his horseflesh requirements. Until Harriet returned, suitably dressed, he had no intention of allowing the lascivious Pasha out of his sight.

Bracelets tinkling on their slender wrists, the dark-skinned girls led Harriet back through the courtyard and into a high-roofed room containing a bath big enough for them all. Already it was being filled by older, plumper women. Harriet's head reeled as she tried to count the number of servants on the Pasha's staff. There had been the uncouth mob who had guided her and Raoul to his presence, the little negro boy, the giggling, chattering girls no older than herself and now even more!

It was obvious that she was to have no privacy in which to bathe. Perfumed oil was poured into the water, flower petals scattered on its surface and then, with much good-natured laughter, the girls began to remove her garments. At first she objected strenuously, but this only increased their hilarity. Eventually, accepting defeat, she removed her dust-stained camisole and underskirt herself. Then she stepped into the luxurious, hot and scented water and unpinned her hair. It fell in a shining mass, rippling over her shoulders and down her back. There were gasps of incredulity and envy, and then she was given soap with which to wash and all the while the girls clustered around the enormous bathtub, chattering and giggling like a flock of brightly coloured birds.

The dust of weeks was rinsed from her hair. She felt clean and fresh but to their dismay adamantly refused the heavy perfumes they plied her with. In vain she looked for her clothes so that she could dress again. There were more giggles. A kaftan of fine, floating silk, delicately embroidered with silver flowers, was held out for her. Velvet slippers replaced the high-button boots. Her hair was still too wet to rebraid and so she left it hanging sleekly down her back, the tendrils around her face curling wispily. Feeling curiously naked she allowed herself to be led once more across the fountain-filled courtyard and into the Pasha and Raoul's presence. At the door the girls hung back and Harriet felt suddenly afraid. Though they had no common language, they had been her own age and friendly. She had disliked the Pasha on sight and was now filled with a sudden dread that when she entered the room, he would be alone; that Raoul would have left in search of the needed horses.

The little negro boy opened the door and hesitantly she entered, her fears subsiding. He had not left her. He was still as she had left him, his white, lavishly laced shirt negligently undone, his close-fitting breeches tucked into sand-covered knee-high boots. He must have ached for a bath as much as she, but he had remained instead with the Pasha. Though not understanding why, she was grateful. The eyes, slanting under winged brows, darkened the instant she stepped into the room. In the loose, flowing kaftan she felt indecently exposed, her small, high breasts pressed tantalisingly against the fine silk.

At the sight of her the Pasha's small pink tongue moved restlessly over his lower lip. The Englishwoman was not only beautiful – she was magnificent. In that moment he determined that however formidable the Frenchman, he would see to it that she never left Berber.

'Send my servant to me,' Raoul demanded abruptly.

Hashim entered, his eyes widening at the sight of Harriet dressed in the manner of one of the Pasha's concubines.

'My cousin needs suitable clothing in which to travel,' Raoul said, his voice throbbing with anger. 'Please see to it.'

Hashim turned obediently, and vainly Harriet wondered where he would obtain the kind of clothes she was accustomed to.

'You must be hot and tired yourself, Capitaine Beauvais,' the Pasha was saying, taking his eyes away from Harriet with difficulty. 'A bath has been prepared . . .'

'Later.' Raoul waved a hand dismissively. 'However, we are both hungry and thirsty.'

Harriet saw the Pasha's eyes narrow malevolently. The man did not like Raoul and no doubt Raoul was aware and uncaring of the fact. Who was he that he could demand hospitality from a man who so clearly disliked him? The rank of captain would not warrant the sort of deference that the Pasha was showing him. Harriet's puzzlement increased as cold meats and fresh fruits were brought in and set on the low table. She remembered the reference to his family name and Raoul's reply that great families had many branches. Who were the Beauvais? Were they a family of stature? Was that the reason he was being treated with such deference?

They sat on velvet cushions to eat, the Pasha half lying, his eyes flicking ceaselessly over Harriet's body. She kept her eyes lowered and ate gratefully, wishing that the company were different. Raoul sat beside her, as at ease on the perfumed cushions as he had been on horseback. She paid little heed to the conversation, only sufficient to understand that the local governor was absent, which was, no doubt, the reason Raoul had sought the Pasha's hospitality instead.

Before the meal was over, there came a deferential knock at the door and at the Pasha's command the little negro boy opened it to reveal a smiling Hashim with a cotton blouse and linen skirt triumphantly laid over his arms, and a pair of thonged sandals in one hand.

Harriet gave a cry of disbelief. Raoul remained infuriatingly unsurprised.

'I would appreciate it if my cousin could change into her own clothes now.' It was not a request. It was an order.

The Pasha flushed angrily but summoned two of the many female observers.

'My cousin is of a very enterprising nature,' Raoul continued, his dark eyes holding Harriet's intently. 'She wishes to see something of Berber before we travel in the morning.'

The Pasha was already rising eagerly to his feet. 'And so my manservant will escort her,' Raoul continued.

'Most unsuitable ... Most ...' The Pasha's eyes met Raoul's. At what he saw there he faltered. Beauvais' reputation was well known in both Egypt and the Sudan. He would have as little regard for the life of a Pasha as he had for a dog in the gutter.

Harriet, not understanding, began to protest, but one glance from Raoul's hard, agate eyes silenced her. Obediently she left the room and freed herself of the perfumed silk. The skirt and blouse were plain and serviceable. She braided her hair and pinned it securely in the nape of her neck. Smoothing the cool linen of the ankle-length skirt, she again felt like Miss Harriet Latimer of Cheltenham. The sandals felt strange at first but were infinitely more comfortable than high-buttoned boots.

When she had changed, Hashim escorted her through the overly rich rooms and she noticed for the first time the curved scimitar at his waist. Two fresh horses waited outside. Hashim shouted what seemed to Harriet to be curses and blasphemies at the many servants who rushed forward to help her mount. They fell back beneath Hashim's onslaught, and he himself helped her into the saddle. She paused as she was exposed once more to the unbearable heat of the afternoon sun.

'I do not really want to see Berber, Hashim.'

He grinned. 'I know that and do not blame you, Miss Harriet Latimer, English lady, but it is my master's wish.'

They cantered towards the dung-filled streets. 'But why, if there is nothing here for me to see?'

He grinned again. 'Maybe not, Miss Harriet Latimer, English lady, but my master wishes to bathe and rest himself.'

'I still don't understand . . .'

Hashim said patiently, 'My master does not trust the Pasha. He is a man who likes women. Many women. My master knows that with me you will be safe.'

Harriet laughed with relief and pleasure. So that was why he had ordered her out into the heat of the afternoon. He had been jealous. It was a novel thought and one she liked. Hashim ignored the cesspool of Berber and rode away from it towards the banks of the river. The broad expanse of water glistened as it swirled onwards towards the coast. She gazed at it in fascination. Where had it come from? Already it was exercising as powerful a hold on her mind as it had on her father's.

'Does anyone know the source of the Nile, Hashim? Do the natives?'

Hashim shook his head. 'It comes from deep in the heart of Africa. From country where no man goes, now or ever.'

'Not even Captain Beauvais?'

Hashim looked at her strangely and dug his heels in his horse's flanks, not answering but riding away from the reed-lined banks and obliging her to follow.

They rode a little way in silence and then Harriet said, 'Why does the Pasha have so many servants? I counted over fifty. Surely he cannot need so many.'

Hashim frowned. 'The Pasha has no servants.'

Harriet said impatiently, thinking that he had misunderstood her, 'Servants, Hashim. The men and women who tend the horses and fetch and carry. The girls who led me away to bathe and change.'

'They are slaves and concubines.'

Harriet gasped, her eyes widening.

'Every Pasha has his slaves and concubines,' Hashim said reasonably.

'But there were scores of them,' Harriet protested.

Hashim shrugged. 'The Pasha is a wealthy man. He can afford to buy many women.'

Harriet felt faint. The girls were no older than herself: some of them younger.

She said in shocked outrage: 'It should not be allowed! It should be outlawed!'

'The English do their best,' Hashim said pacifyingly. 'But it is of little use. In our country there has always been slaves. Why should it suddenly be different?'

'Because it is *wrong* for one human being to belong to another, like a chattel,' Harriet said explosively. 'If I had known I would never have set foot in the Pasha's residence! I would rather have starved!'

This time it was her turn to dig her heels hard into her horse's side.

'Where are you going, Miss Harriet Latimer, English lady?' Hashim called, taken momentarily by surprise at her out burst of rage.

'To Captain Beauvais!' she shouted back over her shoulder. 'I shall tell him immediately of the true state of affairs in the Pasha's residence! Once he knows he will not even spend the night there!'

Hashim sighed, foreseeing trouble in the days ahead. It was patently clear that Miss Harriet Latimer, English lady, knew nothing about the existence in Khartoum of his master's slave. The Circassian – Narinda.

Chapter Three

Harriet rode furiously, her whole being burning with rage. She would tell the Pasha herself what she thought of his domestic arrangements! Berber straddled before her and she reined in, aware that the way back to the Pasha's residence was not as simple as it had seemed. A maze of dust-blown streets and alleyways confronted her. She took the widest and spurred her horse on. It could not be difficult locating a building as grand as the Pasha's. Against the searing blue sky she saw the fluttering flag of the Ottoman Empire and rode confidently towards it. If the Pasha displayed his country's flag so prominently in his main room, then no doubt it also flew from his roof.

Far behind her Hashim saw the route she had taken and rode hard after her, filled with sudden disquiet.

The street narrowed, becoming crowded. Frustratedly Harriet slowed her horse to a walking pace and tried not to let the strange, strong smell overcome her. Wretchedly dressed women halted in their tasks and stared at her in amazement. Children pointed and swarmed around her so that she had to shoo them away, frightened that the smaller one would fall beneath the hooves of her horse. Above the shabby buildings, the red crescent flag fluttered nearer and nearer. At last she turned a corner in its direction and faltered. It did not fly from the Pasha's residence, but from a vast army barracks. Instead of women and children she was suddenly surrounded by men; coarsely dressed, Sudanese soldiers who, the minute they saw her, ran leeringly in her direction. In seconds they had surrounded her, blocking her exit, shouting and laughing at each other in a language incomprehensible to her, but their intent was clear. Desperately she urged the horse forward but scores of hands were holding its head. Other hands, a sea of them, were touching her legs, her waist, trying to unseat her.

'Let go of me! *Let go!*' Frenziedly she lashed out at them with her riding crop, only to arouse a fresh storm of laughter.

Women and children surged from the alleys to watch silently. Hashim was impotent, his horse wedged in on either side by human flesh.

There was a loud scream and above the mass of dark heads he saw Harriet pulled sideways, the horse rearing. Agilely he sprang to the ground and like an eel twisted and pushed through the gathering crowd, not towards Harriet but away, running with the speed of a gazelle in the direction of the Pasha's residence.

'Take your hands off me!' Her voice was a shriek as her riding crop was wrenched from her hand and she was hurled from one pair of searching hands to another.

The men who had crowded her horse had formed a circle and were spinning her from one to another as if she were a rag doll while their less fortunate companions pushed and shoved in order to obtain a better view of the spectacle and gave encouragement by clapping wildly and stamping their feet.

'Stop it! Stop it! Oh let me go, please! Please!'

Her distress only caused more hilarity. The pins in her hair fell free and a great cheer went up as her hair spilled from its prim braids.

Round and round they whirled her so that without the momentum of their hands she would have fallen, sick and dizzy, tears streaming down her face. The noise, the heat, the horror intensified. The buttons were wrenched from her blouse, her heaving breasts contained only by her lace-trimmed camisole.

'No! No!' she gasped. *'Please God. No!'*

Her hair was tugged, wrenching her head back, a triumphant hand seized hold of one of her breasts and in the same split second a revolver shot rang out, scattering the women and children in the alleyways, silencing the beating feet and handclaps of the men.

The hold on her body intensified, brutal fingers digging into the soft flesh. Half senseless, held stationary, the world still spinning about her, Harriet saw the great stallion and its rider force their way through the throng. His shirt was gashed open at the throat as if he had been in the process of dressing when Hashim had reached him. His tightly trousered legs were encased in gleaming Hessian boots; his eyes were frightening, cold and hard, more menacing than the smoking revolver he held in his hand.

The silence was momentary. There were shouts of defiance and abuse from the soldiers and several hands reached to the waists and the pistols lodged there.

'Drop your weapons to the ground or every last one of you will be court martialled and shot!'

The voice was like a whiplash, the authority indisputable.

With shrugs and spits, the men began to disperse, the name Beauvais uttered contemptuously.

Harriet tried to run towards him but could not. The hand securing her breast merely tightened, pulling her hard against an unseen body. From being the centre of a circle, Harriet and her captor now stood alone, the previous participants watching from a safe distance.

Raoul did not even ask that Harriet be set free. From across the dust-filled square he raised the revolver once more, and took careful aim. Harriet's abductor laughed derisively at the gesture and then screamed in pain as his arm was blasted, bone shattering, blood spurting.

Harriet fell forward, sprawling full-length on the mud-beaten ground, her torn blouse seeping with the blood of her assailant.

Shaking convulsively she pushed her tangled hair away from her face and tried to rise to her feet. Through sweat and tears she saw the black boots in front of her, felt strong hands grasp hold of her and lift her in one swift and easy movement into his arms.

A grey-faced Hashim waited in fear as Raoul strode through the square, and, not releasing Harriet, mounted his horse. The men watched silently and sullenly as Raoul's victim rolled and screamed in pain. Hashim felt the hairs on the back of his neck prickle. It would take only one move, one shout of initiative, and the whole pack would be on them. With superb arrogance Raoul rode his horse towards the line that blocked his exit, not pausing for a second as the soldiers showed no sign of giving way. Hashim's fingers tightened around his dagger, and then, as Raoul showed every intention of trampling them underfoot, the crowd parted.

Harriet saw nothing of the silent spectators who watched their progress. Her hair covered her face and breasts, her arms were wrapped around Raoul's lean waist, her head on his chest. When they reached the verdant green of the garden she was still trembling.

Holding her as easily as he would a child, Raoul slid from the saddle and strode through the hordes of excited, chattering servants.

'Malindi!'

A plump woman, some years older than the braceleted girls, stepped forward from the shadows of the courtyard.

'Take care of my cousin for me.'

'Yes, Capitaine Beauvais.'

Her arms tightened around his neck. 'Don't leave me!' Her lips were parted and trembling, her distress palpable.

His voice caught and deepened. 'Have no fear, you will be safe from now on.'

With Malindi hurrying by his side, he carried her across the courtyard and into a suite of cool, high rooms beyond. Behind them Harriet could see the Pasha, flusteredly leading his retinue in an effort to gain pace with them. Raoul continued heedlessly, his indifference to the Pasha's queries and exclamations total. A booted foot kicked open a cane door. Inside was a giant-sized bed, marble figurines, a delicate china wash-bowl and jug, and lush velvet-covered chairs.

As the Pasha breathlessly reached the doorway, mopping his perspiring brow, Raoul laid Harriet down on to unbelievable softness. As he did so her hair fell backwards, the lace of her camisole merely skimming her nipples. Raoul froze, staring down at the purpling imprint of cruel fingers on the delicate flesh. With a swift movement he covered her with a silk sheet and his face terrible, strode from the room.

Harriet tried to rise, calling out his name. Malindi restrained her gently. 'You must sleep, Miss Latimer. You need rest.'

Harriet sank back against the pillows, dazedly aware that she was being addressed by a slave in near-perfect English. Malindi sponged her face and hands with cool water and applied salve to her breast.

'The skin is not broken,' she said comfortingly. 'There will be no infection.'

The strength that had sustained Harriet through her ordeal in the desert, now failed her. She could only murmur her thanks and close her eyes, aware that she was taking help from one of the very slaves she had determined such a little while ago to free.

When she awoke, it was to the light of early morning. Malindi was sitting in a chair, smiling.

'You have slept long and deep.'

'Yes.' She pushed herself up against the pillows.

'I will bring you fresh bread and fruit and coffee.'

As Malindi left the room Harriet swung her legs to the floor. Her breasts throbbed and the purple bruise had deepened, but other than that she felt fit and rested. At the foot of the bed lay a high-necked, full-sleeved blouse. Hashim had been shopping again.

The jug was full of cool, rose-scented water and she washed with pleasure, rebraided her hair, exchanging the torn blouse with the replacement. On the far side of the cane door she saw a dark silhouette and opened it, expecting to see Malindi. Hashim stood there, legs apart and arms folded, his dagger gleaming at his waist. He turned, giving her his blinding, broken-tooth smile.

'You slept well, Miss Harriet Latimer, English lady?'

'Very well, thank you, Hashim. Have you come for me?'

'Come?' He raised scraggy eyebrows. 'Not come. I have been here all night.' He tapped the dagger. 'My master has insisted you be protected at all times.'

Harriet felt a surge of pleasure. 'Where is your master now, Hashim?'

'He is not back yet.'

Harriet's composure fled. 'Back from where?' she cried in alarm.

43

Hashim's grin was buoyant. 'From killing the son of a dog who so abused you.'

Harriet clutched weakly at the door. 'But he left hours ago! Yesterday afternoon!'

'The dog learned of my master's intentions and ran.'

The colour drained from her face. 'Do you mean that Raoul . . . your master . . . is hunting the man down to kill?'

Hashim nodded eagerly. 'But of course. The son of a dog deserves to die. If Allah is good maybe my master will return with his head.'

Harriet pressed her hand to her mouth to stifle a cry of horror. Hashim, misunderstanding her distress, said reassuringly, 'Do not worry, my master has killed many such.'

'But he is a *geographer!*' Harriet protested wildly. 'Not a soldier! Not a murderer!'

'He is a man,' Hashim said simply, and moved aside as Malindi approached with a breakfast tray.

Tremulously Harriet sat once more upon the bed as Malindi poured hot, fragrant coffee and offered her a plate of strange, nearly flat but sweet-smelling cakes. The coffee was reviving; the cakes as delicious as they smelled. She said, when she could trust her voice,

'Has Mr Beauvais returned yet, Malindi?'

'The Capitaine Beauvais arrived five minutes ago. He is bathing and will be ready to leave within the hour.'

The Capitaine. She had heard him addressed as such before. So he *was* more than just a geographer. She remembered the cold, frightening eyes as he had raised his revolver and shot her assailant. It had been the act of a brave, courageous man, for the odds had been overwhelming. Lying in the cool of the room with Malindi at her side, she had marvelled at the fearlessness, the daring, the insolence he displayed towards life. It both aroused and intrigued her. But courage was not hunting down a wounded man with intent to kill. Retribution had already been exacted; there was no need for more.

Hashim had said that Raoul Beauvais had already killed many such. Had she fallen in love with a murderer? A man who held

44

life as cheaply as the slave traders? She shivered. Certainly he was a man held in deep respect. The Pasha's attitude to his guest had shown that quite clearly. Did the respect verge on fear? Why hadn't the soldiers attacked him? Why had they slunk so silently away? They had known who he was. The name Beauvais had been muttered and spat upon. Soldiers, officials, everyone knew of him and who and what he was. Everyone but herself.

There was a light tap at the door and Malindi, fine silk fluttering around her ample body, hastened to open it. It was Hashim.

'My master is ready,' he said simply.

Harriet finished her coffee and rose to her feet, feeling suddenly nervous. At the door she turned and offered Malindi her hand. The older woman took it warmly.

'Goodbye Malindi, and thank you for your care of me.'

'It was a pleasure, Miss Latimer.'

'Malindi . . .?'

'Yes, Miss Latimer.'

'Malindi, where did you learn to speak English so well? The other slaves do not do so.'

Dark grey eyes held hers kindly. 'I am not a slave, Miss Latimer. I am the Pasha's wife.'

Harriet's cheeks flushed as she hastily apologised. Malindi's calm smile deepened. 'It was an understandable mistake, Miss Latimer. One of many that I think you will make. Africa is not an easy land to understand.'

Imperturbably she watched as her husband's concubines descended like pretty butterflies and led Harriet to where Raoul waited.

He was dressed once more as an Arab, his robes shimmering in the morning sunlight, his face half-hidden by his head-dress, only his eyes showing, dark and flashing and unreadable. A scabbard hung at his waist, and the deadly curve of a scimitar gleamed threateningly. She knew that the jewelled dagger would also be on his person; his revolver within easy access in his saddle baggage. They were strange necessities for a man who declared himself to be a mere geographer.

45

The Pasha was looking most unhappy as he wished them a safe journey. Though early in the day, he was perspiring more freely than ever. Harriet took her leave of him with relief. Hashim laughed as they began to canter through the mud-baked streets.

'It is good to see such a man so frightened.'

'Why should the Pasha be frightened?'

Harriet asked curiously.

Hashim laughed again. 'Because my master threatened him with his life.' Harriet's head whirled as she turned to look across at Raoul. 'But why? He was your host. He gave you hospitality.'

They were travelling three-abreast. The broad-brimmed hat that had accompanied her from England had been supplied with fresh veiling that kept the sand and dust from her eyes and mouth. Genie-like, Hashim had procured a parasol and she carried it rolled and tucked down her saddle pack as Raoul and he carried their rifles. It would serve to shield her from the blistering heat later in the day. There was a cool edge to Raoul's voice as he said,

'It was deserved, that is all you need to know.'

'As deserved as your other killings?' Harriet asked, her voice unsteady.

His eyes narrowed. 'Are you criticising my behaviour, Miss Latimer?'

The dam of Harriet's emotions broke. 'Then you do not deny that you have killed men?'

His gaze was disturbingly intense. 'No, Miss Latimer, I do not.'

Tiny green sparks flashed in her eyes. 'Then you are contemptible! Hunting a wounded man down like a dog!'

'Which one of the many men that I have killed are you referring to, Miss Latimer?' There was a hint of menace in his voice that she disregarded.

'The soldier you hunted through the night!'

'Ah. The one who was about to strip you naked and enjoy you publicly before the rest of his companions?'

At his forthrightness Harriet felt her cheeks sting with colour. 'You do not know that . . .'

His hand shot out and grasped the reins of her horse, his voice dangerously quiet. 'I do know that, Miss Latimer. And so do you. Would you have preferred it if I had left him well alone and continued with my bath?'

'I ... No ... I was very grateful ...' His hand had carelessly touched hers and at the heat of it she had started to tremble.

'Then keep your ill-timed comments to yourself.'

She knew that he was conscious of the response of her body to his touch and was furiously angry with herself.

'Your behaviour in wounding him was necessary; killing him was not!'

'I judged that it was.'

She gasped, her eyes widening in horror. 'Then you did kill him?'

He released her horse and stared at her, grim-faced. 'Yes. I killed him.'

'Oh no!' Her eyes were anguished. 'Then you are no better than he! You are a monster! A murderer!'

'I am a bad judge of character,' he agreed tightly. 'Put your missionary heart at rest, Miss Latimer. I did not kill him solely because of his treatment of you. Rather I killed him for a girl who would have been more grateful had she lived. She died three days ago at the same hands that had hold of you. She was twelve years old.'

His whip came down hard on the flanks of his horse and she was left far behind him, shocked and stunned.

Hashim regarded her with something akin to contempt.

'But the Pasha ...' she protested defensively.

Hashim cursed volubly in Arabic. 'The Pasha had arranged for us to be waylaid and for you to be returned to him as a concubine. My master knows well the minds of such men. He bribed the negro boy to tell him his master's plans and then he threatened the Pasha with the blade of his dagger against his throat.' He shrugged. 'There will be no such ambush now.'

Harriet felt as if she were in a world of nightmare.

'But surely, after such treatment, the Pasha will order his men to kill him?'

Hashim's grin returned to his lined and leathery face. 'My master

47

cannot be taken by surprise now and there is no other way to take him. Besides,' he shrugged, 'my master is man of much importance. Such an act would soon be known in Cairo and Alexandria and then what of the Pasha?' He drew a finger across his throat graphically.

Harriet shuddered. She had thought the worst over once the desert had been crossed. Now she realised for the first time that there were other, more menacing dangers than those of nature. There were men like the Pasha; men who were not satisfied with one wife, or even many wives. Men who bought, like cattle, girls to give them pleasure. Men who would kidnap and kill in order to satisfy their bodily lusts. She had seen the way his small, pig-like eyes had followed her every move. She knew only too well that what Hashim said was true. The Pasha *had* planned to have her kidnapped and returned to him and only Raoul had saved her: as he had from the hands of the man he knew to be a perverted killer. She was suffused with shame. She had called him a monster and a murderer, taking no regard of the lawlessness of the country through which they travelled. He alone had stood between her and ravishment. He had promised her protection and had given it, risking his own life in the process. The thanks he had received had been hysterical outpourings more befitting one of her aunts than herself. Miserably she spurred her horse after his, but the strong shoulders remained firmly set against her and when he spoke it was only to Hashim and always in Arabic.

All through the day they travelled, the sand stretched to the horizon on their left, while on their right-hand side, where the Nile flowed, all was green and lush. Dwarf mimosas clustered the banks, palms broke the monotony of the skyline. When they halted for refreshments, Harriet watched incredulously as a family of crocodiles slithered down the river bank and into the water, disturbed by their presence. At dusk they came across a wild herd of asses, and later, as they made camp, she was entranced by the sight of turtles cavorting in the shallows.

None of these pleasures could she share with Raoul. He remained stern-faced and taciturn and not even the appearance of a dhow could pierce her misery.

'It is well on time,' Hashim said with satisfaction and Raoul merely nodded as the lateen-rigged vessel floated nearer and nearer to them.

'Are we not camping here?' she asked Hashim when they were out of Raoul's earshot.

Hashim shook his head. 'We thought we may be until the dhow arrived. But now she is here, we can leave immediately.'

'And sail as far as Khartoum?' Hope filled Harriet's voice.

'Below Shendi, to the sixth cataract. After that . . .' Hashim shrugged.

Harriet wanted to ask how near to Khartoum was the sixth cataract, but a glance from Raoul silenced her. The dhow had anchored near the bank and their horses and baggage were led aboard.

At last he approached her, holding out a hand silently to help her step from the bank to the boat.

Black eyes met green. His grasp on her arm was firm. She said hesitantly, 'I am sorry for the things I said. I did not understand.'

At their feet the velvet-dark waters of the Nile lapped gently. Amongst the reeds small animals scurried, diving softly into the river.

His voice was cool as he repeated Malindi's words. 'Africa is not easily understood,' and then in a voice that brooked no argument, 'that is why it would be best for you to return home at the earliest opportunity.'

She felt tears welling, and fought them down. He would only despise her more if she gave way to them. With the same care he had shown to his animals, he assisted her aboard. She sat at the prow, her hands folded neatly in her lap, her head bowed. She had imagined herself his companion, journeying with him beyond Khartoum. Now she saw herself for what she was. A foolish English girl who annoyed and irritated him; an inconvenience to be got rid of as soon as possible. The dhow skimmed into the centre of the great river. The moon burned high above. Raoul and Hashim

49

spoke in low voices, their heads close together. Harriet's loneliness was absolute. She wanted once more to be called Harriet by him; to be mocked gently; to be the recipient of his rare smiles. Her cheeks scorched. She wanted to be held in strong arms and kissed with indecent thoroughness. She wanted what she could not have. She tilted her chin defiantly. If she was heartbroken, he would not see it. She had pride and that alone would have to sustain her through the coming weeks.

'There is room for you to sleep here undisturbed.' His voice broke in on her thoughts, disinterested, as if it mattered little to him where she slept.

'Thank you.'

Her own voice was cold and stiff, betraying little of the misery she felt. The bunk was barely long enough for her to stretch out on but the small cabin at least afforded privacy.

The dhow sailed steadily towards Khartoum and in her long hours of wakeful restlessness Harriet heard the distant sounds of animals in their nightly hunt for food, and was grateful for the water that separated her from them. Occasionally she heard Raoul's voice and a knife in her heart twisted. Her own private dreams, like her father's, had been reduced to ashes.

She woke to a hot wind carrying the dhow upstream at a brisk pace. Raoul had discarded his Arab dress and was seated on a case of rifles in shirt and breeches, a sheaf of papers spread out before him, working intently. As she emerged into the full blast of the day's heat he raised his head, his eyes meeting hers fleetingly before dropping once more to the notes in his hand.

She picked her way around the crates that littered the deck and sat once more in the prow where she would not have to be constantly moving in order to allow the natives and Hashim to pass as they attended to their tasks.

Hashim brought her a breakfast of flat round cakes and fruit. 'You have not slept well, Miss Latimer, English lady,' he said reprovingly, noting the blue shadows that ringed Harriet's lustrous eyes.

'I am perfectly rested,' Harriet lied, aware that her words could be overheard by the dark, down-bent head.

Hashim frowned, undeceived. English ladies were notoriously difficult to please and he had not relished the companionship of one. However, despite his prejudices, he had come to like Miss Harriet Latimer, English lady, very much. She was courageous and Hashim admired courage. She was also foolish and that he could not understand. Until her denouncement of him as a monster and a murderer, his master too, had admired Miss Harriet Latimer, English lady. Now he treated her as he did all women who sought to gain his attention: with contempt and uninterest. Narinda would have no cause for jealousy when they returned. Hashim was regretful. When his master was not present, the lovely Circassian had the temperament of a shrew and her temper fell upon him often. He would have enjoyed seeing her brought to heel. Now, thanks to Miss Harriet Latimer's incomprehensible attack upon his master, such an occurrence was unlikely. Narinda was already the victor in a battle she was not yet aware of. He felt suddenly sorry for Miss Harriet Latimer, English lady, sitting so lonely and pale-faced, unknowingly returning her rescuer to the arms of a slave girl. With an attempt to bring some animation back into her drawn features, he said,

'There is the mouth of the Atbara.'

He pointed to where a slow running river merged with the waters of the Nile.

Harriet shielded her eyes against the glare of the sun. 'Where does it lead, Hashim?'

'To the mountains of Abyssinia and the home of the Leopard King.'

Harriet smiled. 'Is the Leopard King a man or an animal, Hashim?'

'A man. A very dangerous man. A chieftain who wages permanent war on the Turkish forces. For two years my master mapped the rivers and mountains of the Leopard King's country. It was a task no man had done before.'

Harriet looked across to where Raoul continued to write in a flourishing hand. 'Did not the Leopard King object?'

'To my master?' Hashim asked incredulously. 'My master is not an objectionable man, Miss Harriet Latimer, English lady. He is a man of charm.'

Harriet pursed her lips. If he was, he was concealing the fact most carefully. 'And did your master charm the Leopard King?'

'Most assuredly.'

Once more Harriet allowed her glance to slip across to Raoul. Charm. Threats. He used each one as and when it suited him. She wanted to ask Hashim more. She wanted to ask what had made Raoul Beauvais into such a man. Aware of his nearness she said merely,

'I am sure your master was most at home with warmongering savages.'

Hashim nodded, misunderstanding. Raoul raised his head and she flushed at the contempt on the handsome, strong-boned face. Tears stung her eyes.

She wished she had never met him. She wished he had left her alone in the desert to die. Christian upbringing reasserted itself. No. She did not wish that she was dead. She wished only to recoup her lost dignity.

Hands clasped so tightly in her lap that the knuckles showed white she averted her eyes and stared resolutely at the distant banks of the river. In Khartoum she would no longer have to endure his insolence. In Khartoum she could forget Raoul Beauvais' very existence.

Chapter Four

On the dhow she could not forget him. Wherever she sat he was only a few short steps away, his presence impossible to ignore. The days began to take on an almost domestic routine. The Arabs who had sailed the dhow from Berber worked, ate and slept together in a tight-knit group. Courtesy obliged her to eat Hashim's impeccably prepared food with Raoul, the silence between them marked in contrast to the ceaseless chatter of the Arabs. Harriet endured the daily ordeal with anguish, Raoul with indifference. Every morning, after breakfast, the dhow would moor at the banks of the river and Raoul and a handful of Arabs would combine the exercising of the horses with hunting. His dagger and scimitar had been discarded along with his flowing burnous. In place of loose robes he wore a white linen shirt and Parisian tailored breeches, two silver-mounted pistols in his belt. Seeing the variety of strange beasts that were brought back for Hashim to cook, Harriet found it best not to enquire too closely as to what her meals consisted of. Near starvation in the desert had taught her to be grateful for whatever could be procured.

Through the long, heat-stifling afternoons, Raoul worked, setting his notes in order, revising, correcting. After days of boring monotony Harriet asked him for paper and pen so that she could sketch. There was an almost pleasant curve to his mouth as he acceded to her request. Harriet ignored it. It was too near a smile for comfort. She had come to prefer his disregard. It left her mistress of her emotions.

For hour after hour she sketched the scenes around her; the Arabs as they tended the sails, Hashim squatting over his pots and battered pans, the lovely fluid lines of the dhow, the trees and flowers that crowded the riverbanks, the hippos that the Arabs killed for meat and that tasted extraordinarily good. She was too immersed in her work to be aware of how often or for how long his narrowed eyes rested speculatively on her.

At the sprawling village of Shendi she insisted on the opportunity of taking exercise and walking with Hashim on his quest for whatever provisions were obtainable. The filth and the heat were more overpowering than in Berber and she soon regretted her impulse. When Raoul decided he would also halt the voyage at Matammah so that Hashim could carry out these same errands once again, Harriet expressed no desire to accompany him.

'Are you going to take another stroll?' Raoul asked with infuriating good humour.

'No.' She did not raise her eyes from her sketch pad.

'A pity. Weeks spent without exercise are tedious.'

Her pencil moved furiously over the paper, shading in the outline of Matammah and its crowded streets and buildings of dried river mud. The amusement was back in the strong dark voice; amusement at her discomfort. The lines of her jaw tensed as she strove to remain calm. Whatever else she did, she would not give him the satisfaction of seeing how his amusement enraged her.

'Perhaps you would like to ride when we exercise the horses?'

There was nothing she would have liked to do more. She said coolly, 'No, thank you.'

The corner of his mouth quirked in a suppressed smile. He had determined to have nothing further to do with her. Her ridiculous outburst over his killing of the brute who had been on the verge of raping her had angered him beyond all measure. It had not been the reaction he had expected. In the days that had passed since then his anger had simmered and cooled. Miss Harriet Latimer did not react predictably in any situation. It was the reason she afforded him such secret delight. She should have been appalled by the swarms of half-clad Arabs manning the dhow, and had not been. She should have turned distastefully away from the strange concoctions emerging from Hashim's cooking pot and had not done so. She should have been petulant at her self-imposed incarceration in the prow and instead had busied herself sketching. The sketches had been another surprise.

When she had left the dhow at Shendi in Hashim's company, he had leafed through them, expecting to see the tedious attempts at art that all well-brought-up young ladies aspired to. Instead he had found strong, evocative sketches of scenery and portraits of Hashim and the Arabs that caught every nuance of movement. There were none of himself. He had slid them back into order aware that Miss Harriet Latimer was taking up more and more of his thoughts. At Berber he had categorised her as a female nuisance, conveniently forgetting the stamina and courage she had displayed in the desert. Now he was faced with other aspects of her character: she was talented, resourceful and blessedly uncomplaining. Her quick retorts and defiantly tilted chin only served to amuse him. He knew very well that she ached to ride and that only pride prevented her from accepting his offer. He did not try to press her. Instead, when he returned from his own ride the next morning, he stretched luxuriously, declaring to Hashim that the ride had been both invigorating and enjoyable. Harriet's chin had tilted a degree fractionally higher and he had surveyed her with a gleam in his eyes as he drank a refreshing glass of lime juice.

After two such mornings he said idly, 'The Arab who rides your horse has turned his ankle. I would be obliged if you could exercise him yourself this morning.'

Harriet's delicate jawline tightened. 'I have told you, Mr Beauvais, I have no desire for exercise.'

'Maybe not, Miss Latimer, but the horse has.'

Disguising the flood of pleasure the prospect of riding gave her, Harriet set her sketch pad to one side and said coolly, 'Very well, Mr Beauvais. If it is a necessity.'

He slid his pistols through the broad leather of his belt and handed her a small, double-barrelled gun. Harriet backed away distastefully.

'No thank you, Mr Beauvais. I do not share your appetite for killing.' Her green-gold eyes were withering. He fought down a hot flush of anger and said curtly,

'The gun is for your protection, not your pleasure. The animals roaming the banks are not converted to pacifism.'

Unwillingly her hand closed around the butt of the gun.

'It is a Fletcher,' he said as she stared at it in dislike. 'You will find it easier to handle than a rifle.'

'I shall not be handling it, Mr Beauvais.'

He shrugged and mounted his horse agilely, leaving Hashim to assist her into the saddle. The horse felt strange beneath her. She had to ride astride like a man, for she had no riding dress. Too late she remembered her lack of horsemanship and hoped that the horse would understand and be amenable. More fervently still, she hoped that her inexperience would not be apparent to Raoul Beauvais.

They cantered through groves of acacias and not until the wide river was obscured by verdant wilderness did Harriet realise they were alone. The Arabs who usually accompanied him had all remained behind. She wondered if he had known they would do so before they set off, and if so, what his purpose was in riding alone with her. Certainly it was not for companionship, for he rode a little way ahead, his lean muscled body remote and unapproachable.

She dismissed the absent Arabs from her mind and concentrated instead on her mount. The ponies she had ridden in Cheltenham had not been preparation for an Arabian mare. Yellow hot rocks interspersed the shrubs and trees and through the hanging foliage Harriet could see the barren wastes that lay beyond the greenness of the Nile's banks. Her horse was growing increasingly restless and Raoul turned, his brows meeting in a deep frown. After another few yards he reined in, his body taut with tension. With difficulty Harriet reined her horse alongside him.

'What is it? What's the matter?'

He silenced her with a swiftly raised hand, listening intently. Harriet could hear nothing, yet not only her horse but also Raoul's was champing at the bit, ears pricked with fear. She saw Raoul's hand reach down for his pistol and felt a trickle of cold sweat in the nape of her neck. The silence was eerie. The birds that had been darting overhead had scattered with loud cries of alarm. Only the vibrating leaves testified to their recent presence.

'I think . . .' Raoul began in a low voice, and then Harriet shrieked as her mare reared, hooves flailing.

She saw Raoul's hand shoot out for the reins and miss by inches as the terrified mare broke into a headlong gallop. Her feet slipped from the stirrups; she was slithering helplessly in the saddle, sand and stones, shrubs and creepers a whirling blur as she struggled to stay mounted. The reins, hung loose and her arms circled the mare's sweating neck, her face pressed close into the mane as it raced heedlessly towards the desert. Through her terror she was dimly aware of Raoul's shout and the thunder of following hooves and then the mare leapt over an obstacle and her hand clasp broke. There was a split-second kaleidoscope of sun and sky and then she hit the ground and lay lifeless.

She tried to breathe and could not. Her chest felt as if it were in a vice. Through a blood-red mist she heard Raoul calling her name and then there was daylight again and she was saying stupidly,

'I fell.'

He was holding her tightly, burying his head in her hair. She could feel him shaking as he held her close against him, and dazedly wondered what he was doing kneeling in the sand, his composure gone, his eyes black pits in an ashen face. Tentatively she raised her hand and touched his cheek.

'Are you all right?' she asked, her breath coming easier, the pain in her back and chest receding.

'Yes.' He looked down at her, his voice thickening. At what she saw in his eyes desire surged through her like a flame.

'No . . .' she protested weakly, and then closed her eyes in surrender as he kissed her long and deeply. She could no more help responding to him than she could help breathing. Her arms slid up and around him, her kisses as burning, as passionate, as his own. When at last he raised his head from hers there was incredulity on his face.

'*Mon Dieu*,' he said softly, gazing down at the heart-shaped face, the gentle, sweet, sensuous lips, the green-gold eyes that tormented him waking and sleeping.

'I . . . it was an accident . . . the fall,' she began, colour flooding her cheeks.

The incredulity had vanished to be replaced by a strange gleam in eyes she saw were as black in sunlight as they were in shadow. So this was how his days of bachelorhood were to end. Tumbling in the sand with a Miss scarce out of the schoolroom.

'The accident be damned,' he said huskily, kissing her again with increasing passion.

Wild joy surged through her. They were once again as they had been before Berber. She loved him with all her heart and her kisses left him in no doubt of it.

When at last he raised his head from hers he gazed down at her wonderingly. 'You did not even have your hair unpinned, *chérie*,' he said, a smile tugging at the corners of his mouth.

'I will wear it unpinned all day long if it pleases you,' she said shyly.

He tightened his hold of her. 'That pleasure is for my eyes alone. Not for Hashim and a dozen Arabs.'

She flushed. 'Do you care for me so much?'

His white teeth flashed in a sudden smile. He was damned if he was going to propose marriage in the middle of the desert. 'Very much,' he said and lifted her gently to her feet. Her face was radiant as he caught hold of the reins of the horse.

He loved her as much as she loved him. She could tell by the expression in his eyes, the tone of his voice.

He helped her into the saddle and said thickly, 'I thought you were dead, *ma petite*.' Her eyes sparkled as his arms circled her waist. 'I thought I was dead, too.'

'You are very much alive, *chérie*,' he said, prodding the horse to a canter. 'More alive than anyone else I've ever met.'

She nestled close against his chest as the acacias thinned and the sails of the dhow shone brightly in the sun. 'Why did my horse bolt?' He hesitated fractionally and then said, 'It was fear. Probably of the animal I heard and did not see.'

'And what will happen to her? Will you be able to find her?'

'There is no need.' He pointed towards the dhow. 'She has already returned home.'

'Oh!' Harriet stared to where Hashim was busily rubbing the steaming mare with cloth. 'Isn't she clever?'

'More than you know,' he said cryptically, swinging her to the ground.

Hashim looked from Harriet's glowing face to his master's and then back again. So ... Narinda would have cause for jealousy after all.

'Are we ready to sail now, Effendi?' he asked, continuing with his task.

Raoul handed his horse to one of the Arabs and stared thoughtfully at the bank. 'Yes, Hashim. The sooner the better.'

Harriet moved into the prow as the Arab sailors began to guide the dhow once more into mid-stream.

'What happened, Effendi? Why did Miss Harriet Latimer, English lady's mare bolt?' Hashim asked in a low voice.

'A lion,' Raoul said so that no one but Hashim could hear. 'I'm almost certain it was a lion.'

'So far north?' Hashim asked incredulously.

Raoul nodded. 'I didn't see him, but I could almost smell him.'

'Then Miss Harriet Latimer, English lady, is fortunate at having such a hunter with her to protect her.'

A slight smile curved Raoul's lips. *Mon Dieu*, but they had nearly both died. The sight of Harriet's seemingly lifeless body had driven all thoughts of the lurking lion from his consciousness. He had been possessed of a far more terrifying fear. His pulse beat quickened as he remembered her response to his kisses. If his instinct had been right, and there had been a lion in the vicinity, then they had been fortunate that it had not been a hungry one. He shook his head in disbelief. What sort of passion drove the thought of such a predator from a man's mind? He looked across to where Harriet was sketching demurely, her wide-brimmed hat shading her eyes, her lips pursed in concentration.

'*Mon Dieu*,' he said again to himself. 'After all these years! To be ensnared by a missionary's daughter!'

He began to laugh and Hashim regarded him curiously. Lions were no laughing matter. What, then, was?

'I have a confession to make to you,' Harriet said as the blood-red sun sank behind the skyline and the dhow continued gently upstream. They had just finished their evening meal, a stew of pigeon and quail that had been pleasingly appetising.

'Tell me,' Raoul said as she leaned against him and his fingers touched the softness of her hair. 'Confession is good for the soul.'

'You are teasing me again.'

'I am not.' His deep, dark eyes held concealed laughter. 'I just cannot imagine what wicked sin you could possibly have to confess.'

'It isn't a sin . . . At least, I don't think so.'

Her skin gleamed palely in the moonlight, her face troubled. His laughter faded.

'Tell me, *chérie*. What is it that troubles you so?'

'I am afraid it may have been my fault that my mare bolted, and not that of a nearby animal. You see . . .' Her fingers twisted in her lap. '. . . I am not a horsewoman and I should have told you so.'

He rocked her gently in his arms, the most curious tenderness sweeping through him.

'It was not your fault, *ma chérie*. Do not worry about not being a good horsewoman. I will teach you. We will ride together every morning and evening.'

His eyes met hers and travelled to her lips. Harriet felt her nerves begin to throb. Vainly she thought of her aunts and of how horrified they would be if they knew of her behaviour. Vainly she thought of her father: tried to summon the willpower to turn her head away, to reprove him for his conduct. Instead, she heard herself give a cry of breathless joy as his head moved down, kissing the hollow of her throat. His touch seared her. It was as though he had a right to her body, as though the intimacy of their embrace was pre-ordained. His hands caressed her breasts and she moaned softly, the fever possessing her rising higher and hotter.

He tensed, steeling himself until he was rigid. She was eighteen; a wide-eyed innocent pagan. He was thirty-two, worldly and, according to the opinion of some, dissolute. His desires could be indulged no further without matrimony. He said, with a crooked smile,

'You need a chaperon, Miss Latimer.'

She leaned against him, extremely happy, extremely confident.

'I shall have one in Khartoum, Mr Beauvais,' and did not see the sudden darkening in his eyes at her words.

Khartoum. She still had no idea of what she would find there. It was his duty to warn her. He said awkwardly,

'Harriet . . .' and got no further.

Hashim approached, a lantern held high in his hand.

'I can hear cataracts, Effendi.'

Raoul frowned and removed his arm from Harriet's slender shoulders. 'At this time of the year it should be no problem. We should be able to sail them.'

'The Arabs do not think so, Effendi.'

Raoul rose to his feet. 'Then I had better speak to them.'

From then until they reached Khartoum Raoul supervised the sailing of the dhow himself. Harriet, aware that she could best help him by keeping out of the way, spent her days curled up in the prow, sketching furiously.

The scenery that had been so bleak on leaving Berber had changed considerably. Now the river was dotted with a whole succession of islands, so many that the Arabs declared there were ninety-nine of them and Harriet spent her time counting to see if it was true. Groves of holy thorn overhung with flowering creepers crowded the shoreline so that it resembled a luxurious green wilderness.

The Nile altered character, plunging through narrow straits that reduced it to a deep mountain stream and then spreading broadly again as it approached its junction with its main tributary, the Blue Nile, that flowed from the Abyssinian mountains, and the home of the Leopard King.

Would he return to those distant highlands? Would she accompany him as his wife? She hugged her sketch pad to her breast, feeling a warm glow suffuse her. As his wife she would accompany him wherever he chose, whether it be to the lands of the Leopard King or deeper into unexplored Africa; a return to Cairo or Alexandria; or a return to his home in France. Wherever he went, his destination would be hers also.

'Khartoum,' he said, striding towards her, his lean, muscled body damp with sweat beneath his linen shirt. 'You are as far south now as any European woman has ventured.'

'It looks very agreeable.'

'Distance lends enchantment. It's a cesspool of vice and corruption.'

Her smile was impish. 'Then as a missionary's daughter, I shall have to reform it.'

'You will remain untouched by it,' he said, and she was startled by the depth of feeling in his voice. 'The degradation of Khartoum is beyond your comprehension.'

'Yet Hashim says you have a permanent residence in the city.'

'I have.' His voice was strangely curt. 'However, it is not a residence suitable for yourself. You will stay with Lady Crale as your father wished.'

Her heart began to beat irregularly and she was filled with sudden apprehension. 'And you will visit me there?'

His quick smile reassured her.

'I will see you there,' he said and swung on his heel, calling out instructions in Arabic as the dhow threatened to become entangled in a flotilla of smaller boats, all converging on the white-walled city. Harriet regarded it with interest. It looked far more pleasant than Berber. Palms and tropical fruit trees sprung up between the closely-packed houses. The riverside was lush and verdant, domes and minarets dotted the skyline, their cupolas gleaming dull gold in the sun. Altogether, it looked most pleasing.

The Arab sailors swarmed over the side as the boat moored, whooping with glee, scampering into the crowds that thronged the streets.

'Worthless dogs,' Hashim said, shaking his fist after them.

Raoul grinned. 'They'll be back. They have yet to be paid.'

He was looking down at her, and a little pulse began to beat wildly in her throat as he took her hand.

'Hashim will accompany you to Lady Crale.'

'But I thought you would be accompanying me . . .'

'I have business to attend to. I will call you tomorrow.'

'But . . .'

He swung her up in his arms and carried her ashore, setting her down amidst noisy, shouting traders.

'Tomorrow,' he said, and his voice brooked no contradiction.

Fighting her disappointment, she watched as he summoned a dust-covered and battered carriage. 'Hashim will take care of you.' He raised her fingers to his lips and kissed them. '*Au revoir*, my love.'

Hashim sat beside her, glowering ferociously at those who had the temerity to stare at the slender English girl with the sun-gold hair.

Harriet was oblivious of the stares of the curious. As their horse-drawn carriage trundled rapidly away from the riverside and towards the centre of the city, she looked behind her, waving until his tall, powerful figure could no longer be seen.

Close to the hot bustling streets were not as attractive as they had seemed. The city smelt of dust and dung and the air was heavy with the strange sounds of muezzins calling the faithful to prayer and the barking of pi-dogs and the ceaseless thud of camel hooves.

Why had he not come with her? What business could be so important that he would entrust the supervision of her meeting with Lady Crale to the hands of Hashim? Oddly deflated, Harriet tried to summon some enthusiasm for the coming interview. At least, thanks to her father, she was expected. She would be in the home of a fellow countrywoman and not exposed to the likes of the Pasha.

The carriage jolted uncomfortably to a halt before an imposing white-walled residence. Picking up her skirts, she stepped cautiously down and waited with increasing nervousness as Hashim rang at the gateway for admittance.

A sleekly groomed Arab answered the summons. Angry words

were exchanged between them. Harriet's anxiety grew. Surely Raoul should have foreseen such difficulties? Why, oh why, could he not have accompanied her? With Raoul at her side she would not have been apprehensive. She could have faced a dozen Lady Crales with impunity.

Eyes flashing dangerously, Hashim turned to her. 'This son of a dog will not permit me to enter with you until he has spoken to his mistress.'

The iron gate closed against them. The heat was stifling, Harriet wiped her brow, feeling both humiliated and undignified. The Arab returned and sulkily admitted them. Hashim crowed triumphantly over him and then surveyed the splendid inner courtyard with admiration. There was a pond and a fountain that far exceeded in size and grandeur the residence of the Pasha.

White and blue water lilies floated gently on the surface. Coral-red aloes and bright orange ambatch plants filled the square with brilliant colour. Giant fig trees and wild-date palms gave shade. Hot stone gave way to cool tiles. Hashim had dropped a respectful distance behind her. There was no sign of braceleted, dark-eyed girls as there had been at the Pasha's. Lady Crale's servants were attired in uniform, a silk sash crossing their breasts, turbans on their head. One set of folded doors opened after another. The furnishings were entirely English. There was no hint of Africa in the plush upholstered armchairs and glass cabinets of books.

'My dear child!' A statuesque woman with kind eyes and warm smile was hurrying towards her, petticoats rustling beneath a blue gown. 'How unexpected your arrival is! I have had no word from your father for months. Do sit down and take tea.' A cool hand clasped Harriet's and guided her towards a velvet-upholstered chair. 'What an ordeal your journey must have been! I warned your father as to the wisdom of it, but he would not be dissuaded. He was insistent that you were strong enough for the rigours of the desert and so you have proved. Nevertheless, I shall take him to task for worrying me so.' She gazed expectantly at the still-open door.

'My father is not with me, Lady Crale.'

64

'Not with you!' Lady Crale swung round aghast. 'My dear child, what do you mean?'

Tears filled Harriet's eyes. 'I am afraid that my father is dead, Lady Crale.'

Lady Crale's face paled. She reached out her hand, grasping the back of a chair to steady herself. 'Dead! But where? How?' Dazedly she walked across the room and sat down.

'In the desert. Tribesmen stole our baggage camels and we were left without provisions.'

'But this is terrible, terrible.' Lady Crale stared across at Harriet horrified. 'Your father was such a good man. He accomplished so much in Cairo and was eager to do the same here. Oh, it does not bear thinking of!'

Harriet's eyes were bright with tears. 'I do not think he suffered much pain in the end. He was overcome with exhaustion and death came swiftly.'

'Poor, dear child.' Lady Crale reached out and clasped Harriet's hand in her own. 'What agonies you have suffered.' Her eyes changed expression. 'But how did you cross the desert without companions or stores?' she asked curiously. 'How have your reached Khartoum?'

Harriet remembered the lie Raoul had told the Pasha in order to protect her reputation. That she was his cousin. It was a lie that could be dispensed with now. In another few days she would be his wife and that would surely silence any unkind tongue.

'I was rescued by a naturalist and a geographer travelling south.'

Relief and horror fought for mastery on Lady Crale's finely-drawn features. 'My dear child. Are you telling me you have travelled from the Nubian Desert accompanied only by two gentlemen?'

'By one gentleman,' Harriet corrected, a smile curving her lips. Lady Crale pressed a hand against her palpitating heart. 'But this is dreadful! Why, anything could have happened to you! You could have been . . . Have been . . .'

'Mr Beauvais is a Frenchman and a gentleman of much standing in Cairo and Alexandria,' Harriet said, attempting to set Lady Crale's fears at rest.

'Beauvais?' Lady Crale murmured, a travesty of the cool, assured

65

woman who had greeted her only moments before. 'Did you say Beauvais?'

'Yes. Mr Raoul Beauvais. He has a house in Khartoum. Are you acquainted with him?'

Lady Crale's face was deathly. 'Smelling salts,' she gasped weakly, gesturing in the direction of a rosewood secretaire.

Hastily Harriet rose and sought out the smelling salts. It had not occurred to her that Lady Crale would be so overcome by the news of her father's death.

'There is no reason to distress yourself, Lady Crale,' she said solicitously, as she pressed the salts into a trembling hand. 'My father died in the country he loved and would have preferred that to dying in his bed at Cheltenham.'

'Yes. Of course.' Lady Crale attempted to rally herself.

'As for myself, I have been most fortunate and am very grateful for the fact.'

Slight colour had returned to Lady Crale's cheeks. 'You are, of course, welcome to stay here for as long as you desire, Harriet. However, it may be best if arrangements are put in hand for you to return to Cairo and thence to England, *suitably* escorted of course. Such arrangements can be difficult to make and can take time. Unfortunately, the consul is absent at the moment.'

'Please don't worry about me, Lady Crale. I am sure that things will sort themselves out most satisfactorily.'

Prudence warned her against telling Lady Crale that she would be marrying Raoul Beauvais and would no longer need her protection. Such news would best come from Raoul himself.

Lady Crale summoned the strength to ring the bell at her side. 'My maid will show you to the room that has been set aside for you. No doubt you will need a rest after your ... your trials.'

Harriet turned to say 'goodbye' to Hashim but the large room was empty except for themselves.

'Is something amiss, Harriet? You don't mind me calling you Harriet, do you? "Miss Latimer" sounds so cold and formal and in all my correspondence with your dear father you were referred to as "Harriet" and so I have come to know you.'

'I much prefer "Harriet" to "Miss Latimer",' Harriet said truthfully. 'I was looking for Hashim.'

'Beauvais' servant? Don't worry about him. He will be given a cooling drink before returning to his master.'

It seemed strange to hear Hashim referred to as a servant and not a friend. Disappointedly, she waited for the arrival of the maid and then followed her up a shallow flight of stone stairs to a simply, but comfortably, furnished bedroom. Only later, when she had washed and changed into fresh clothes provided by Lady Crale, did it occur to her that it was stranger still that Lady Crale should refer to Raoul as simply 'Beauvais'. No doubt she had misheard. Such rudeness would be uncharacteristic of a lady who was obviously both kind and thoughtful.

From the balcony of her room Harriet could see the Nile, pelicans and great maribou storks thronging the dun-coloured water. Beyond the banks there was nothing but desert stretching to the horizon on either side.

She wondered where Raoul was: if his Khartoum house was similar to Lady Crale's; if it was nearby. Perhaps, even now, he was only a short distance from her.

She stepped inside and closed the shutters, lying on the bed and watching the motes of dust dance in the fierce shafts of sunlight that slanted through the wooden slats. Tomorrow they would be able to talk without Hashim or the sailors overhearing. Tomorrow he would make his intentions clear. He would inform Lady Crale that he wished to marry her and from then on their courtship would be regularised. She smiled and closed her eyes. He had still to ask her to marry him. No doubt he thought such a question irrelevant: her arms and lips had already told him of her answer.

Lady Crale had changed into a dinner dress of emerald silk. Diamonds sparkled at her wrist and throat. A thousand miles from civilisation, she looked as if she was entertaining in her London home in Bloomsbury Square.

'There will be five of us for dinner, Harriet. Dr Walther, a German and a most interesting gentleman. His daughter, Magdalene – she is a year or two your senior, but will be very pleased at having you for a companion; and my son, Sebastian.' She patted her elaborate coiffure, once more poised and in control of the situation. 'I think it best, Harriet, if you do not mention the manner in which you arrived in Khartoum. The European population here is small and it may be . . . misunderstood.'

The gown that the maid had laid out for Harriet was a deep rose-pink with a nipped-in waist and a fashionable décolleté neckline. Over hoops, the crinoline skirt surged and billowed and Harriet found it hard to believe that she was in Africa and not at a smart evening party in Cheltenham. Only the daring plunge of the neckline assured her that it was not so. Modesty overcame fashion in Cheltenham. Such a neckline on a girl of eighteen would never have been countenanced.

Lady Crale's kindness had been overwhelming and if her unchaperoned journey to Khartoum was likely to cause embarrassment, then Harriet saw no reason to talk of it. All such difficulties would be resolved with Raoul's arrival.

In the dining room silver gleamed on white napery. Small negro boys wafted the air with long ostrich feathers. Dr Walther and his daughter were introduced to Harriet, the Doctor's eyes warmly welcoming and incurious, his daughter's sharply feline. With the arrival of Sebastian Crale Harriet understood the reason for her cold reception from the other girl. Sebastian Crale was in his mid-twenties and undeniably dashing. His fair hair shone sleekly, his moustaches impeccably trimmed. His eyes were an arresting grey and his well-shaped mouth smiled easily and often.

Magdalene's eyes followed his every move and Harriet was disconcerted as Sebastian Crale gave her his undivided attention throughout dinner, his manner blatantly appraising. She wanted to tell Magdalene that she had no cause for concern; that she had no intention of ensnaring Sebastian Crale; that her heart was given elsewhere and that in another few hours she would be affianceed.

A slight frown furrowed Lady Crale's brow but otherwise she gave no indication that she found her son's open admiration of Henry Latimer's daughter disturbing. She had smoothly explained to her guests that Harriet had been escorted by friends to Khartoum and would be staying at the consulate.

'It is an amazing journey from the coast to Khartoum, do you not think so, Miss Latimer?' the little German asked, wiping his rimless spectacles on his table napkin.

'It is extremely boring,' Magdalene said before Harriet could reply. 'Why Papa insists on remaining here I cannot imagine. We have a large establishment in Stuttgart and a magnificent summer house in the Bavarian Alps. Do you like Bavaria?' she asked, turning to Sebastian as the servants placed iced soup before the guests.

'A lovely city,' Sebastian replied, gazing at sleekly coiled gold braids.

'*Bavaria!*' Magdalene hissed, her cat eyes feral as she failed to gain his attention.

'Oh yes, of course.' He did not trouble to turn towards her.

Where on earth had his mother's guest sprung from? His mother had told him that she was a missionary's daughter but he found it hard to believe. Her grace and poise were effortless. His mother was no doubt trying to dissuade him from another emotional entanglement. He tried to think who was in Cairo and Alexandria. The Duke and Duchess of Stathlone had been there recently. Had they any adventurous daughters? He didn't recall that they had. Fish followed the soup. Whoever she was, she was captivating. He drank his chilled wine thoughtfully. Beauvais would know; Beauvais knew everything.

'Did you know Raoul Beauvais arrived this afternoon?' he asked the table at large. 'Things should move pretty fast now.'

'I am surprised to hear you speak his name,' Magdalene said viciously. 'The man is a dissolute renegade.'

'Dissolute, certainly,' her father said, 'but he does not deserve the name of renegade.'

Harriet could hardly believe her ears. Her eyes flashed fire. 'He does not deserve any such names!' she said furiously, setting down her knife and fork and glaring at them. 'He is a courageous man: a gentleman. He has been very kind to me and I will not allow him to be vilified in such a wicked manner.'

Lady Crale closed her eyes and sank visibly in her chair. Dr Walther, Magdalene and Sebastian regarded her with astonishment.

'Beauvais has never been kind to a woman in his life,' Sebastian managed at last. 'He wouldn't know how.'

'They say he's kind to his little slave girl,' Dr Walther chuckled.

Magdalene shivered in distaste. Harriet stared incredulously at Dr Walther.

'Slave? Are you trying to tell me that Raoul Beauvais has slaves?'

'*Everyone* in Khartoum has slaves,' Sebastian said easily. 'Only others do not flaunt the fact like Beauvais does.'

'Certainly they do not parade their native mistresses in public,' Dr Walther agreed.

Harriet felt the blood leave her face. There was a pounding in her ears so that she could hardly hear her own voice as she asked,

'Mistresses?' Her eyes dilated, her breath coming in harsh gasps.

'Dr Walther is unfair to him,' Sebastian said, drinking more wine. 'Beauvais has only one. The Circassian – Narinda.'

Chapter Five

From the head of the table there came a groan as Lady Crale reached weakly for her glass. Harriet was oblivious of it. The whole world seemed to have shifted on its axis. The faces around her jumped and danced; the walls of the dining room were closing in on her.

'Are you feeling all right?' Sebastian Crale was asking with concern.

Dr Walther was urging a glass of water upon her.

'I . . . Yes . . .' She pressed a hand to her throbbing temple.

Lady Crale rose smoothly in a rustle of skirts. 'Miss Latimer has undergone a most arduous journey. I should have realised that she needed to rest for a much longer period. Jali! Hasara! Kindly accompany me to Miss Latimer's room.'

A firm but kindly hand was placed beneath Harriet's elbow. Dazedly she allowed Lady Crale to help her to her feet. Her hostess was saying smoothly,

'It was most remiss of me to expect Miss Latimer to endure a dinner party in her weakened condition. If you will excuse us Magdalene, Dr Walther . . .'

With the decorously dressed Sudanese maids hurrying in her wake, Lady Crale escorted Harriet from the dining room and towards her bedroom.

'I'm sorry . . . I've ruined your dinner party . . .' Inbred politeness asserted itself.

'Nonsense. It was I who was at fault expecting you to be strong enough for such a social occasion when you have scarcely had time to rest after your arrival.'

As Lady Crale removed her steadying arm, Harriet staggered towards the bed and sank down heavily. She looked ghastly. Her delicately-boned, heart-shaped face was pinched and drawn. The eyes that had sparkled with such delight at the sight of the rose-pink gown, were now glazed with shock and lustreless.

Lady Crale tightened her lips. She had feared the worst when Harriet had told her the identity of her rescuer. Raoul Beauvais was a man shunned by all decent society.

For two years he had lived quite openly with a slave girl as his mistress. He had even had the effrontery to enter European homes with her as his guest. He had offended every lady of sensibility and every gentleman of honour. Only his illustrious family name had saved him from complete ostracism. His personal wealth far exceeded that of a British consul and reduced the vast riches of the Turkish Governor-General to a seemingly trifling amount. It was rumoured that he was a personal friend of Emperor Napoleon III and certainly the authorities in Cairo and Alexandria held him in high esteem. Lady Crale shuddered. *They* were not insulted by being presented to a native as if she were an equal. She had heard whispers as to the indecencies that took place behind the high walls of Raoul Beauvais' Khartoum residence. The Circassian was displayed openly: how many others were kept in secret?

Lady Crale was not an unworldly woman. She had accompanied her husband to many remote and uncivilised corners of the globe. To India and Afghanistan; to the Levant and to Africa. In the course of her travels she had met adventurers, renegades, rogues and free-booters. In her opinion, Raoul Beauvais fell into all four categories. Unfortunately he had two qualities that none of the others had possessed. He was fiendishly handsome and his charm, when he chose to exert it, was phenomenal. It was hardly surprising that the gently-reared missionary's daughter should have fallen victim to it. Nor, taking into consideration Harriet's own charms, was it surprising that Beauvais should have sought to take advantage of her vulnerable position. A dark, unspeakable thought entered Lady Crale's mind. *Had* he taken advantage of it? The sensual

Frenchman had been alone with Harriet for several weeks. She sank weakly onto the bed beside Harriet.

What she was thinking was impossible, monstrous. Harriet Latimer was an English girl; not a Circassian who could be bought for twenty pounds. She said, striving to keep her voice calm,

'I had hoped to spare you the kind of conversation you heard this evening. It was for that reason that I deemed it best you did not announce the name of your companion.'

'But it can't be true!' Harriet turned to her, wild-eyed, and Lady Crale's apprehension grew. 'Mr Beauvais is a man of honesty and integrity! He would not keep slaves! He would not make mistresses of them!'

'I am afraid that the latter is beyond dispute, Harriet. The Circassian has enjoyed and occupied that position in Mr Beauvais' household for over two years now. It is known all over the Sudan.'

'*No!*' Revulsion flooded through Harriet. 'I refuse to believe it! There has been a mistake! A misunderstanding!'

'The European society in Khartoum is small,' Lady Crale said firmly. 'There can be no mistaking the manner in which Mr Beauvais has publicly paraded the girl in question. Certainly there can be no mistaking that he bought her as a slave. He did so in full view of half Khartoum's population.' She paused. She was accustomed to being silent on such matters but the circumstances called for frankness. She said, 'Circassians are rare in Khartoum. The slaves auctioned are usually from the interior – Dinkas or Shiluks. The unfortunate creatures are bought by trades and transported to the coast. However, a few are sold into service here in Khartoum.' She paused delicately. 'Especially the girls if they are at all pretty. The Turkish officials in Khartoum are not in the habit of being accompanied by their wives. It makes for . . . regrettable behaviour.'

Bile rose in Harriet's throat. 'I have already come into contact with that side of life in Africa,' she said through parched lips. 'In Berber, at the home of the Pasha.'

'Then you will appreciate that what I am telling you is the truth. It is British policy to put an end to the slave trade. The attempt to do so occupies a vast amount of my husband's time. Your dear father fought valiantly against the practice in Cairo and would have done so here in Khartoum if he had lived. Of course, the Turkish Governor-General denies knowing anything about the slaves that are auctioned publicly, day in and day out. We have not, and can never hope to receive help in stamping out the abomination from such a source. The Turkish garrison in the town is composed almost entirely of Sudanese natives: natives who have been bought. Malaria constantly depletes their numbers and the garrison can only be kept at full strength by resorting to such measures.'

'It is unspeakable,' Harriet said, hugging her folded arms close to her breast. 'I accept all that you tell me about slavery in Khartoum, Lady Crale. But one thing I cannot accept is that the Circassian is either Raoul Beauvais' slave or his mistress.'

'Circassian slaves are very rare and very beautiful,' Lady Crale said, a tiny spot of colour in her cheeks. 'The bidding for the girl called Narinda was extraordinarily high. An aide of the governor's was determined to have her and outbid all the local traders. A large crowd had gathered by the time Raoul Beauvais stunned the European community by openly bidding against the Turk. Of course, Mr Beauvais is a Frenchman, not an Englishman, but his behaviour could only attract scandal. The girl was, and is, exquisite, and every man there knew the reason why Beauvais and the Turk were bidding so high a price for her.'

Harriet felt as if the breath was being squeezed, inch by inch, from her body. 'No,' she repeated in vain again. 'It cannot be. It is impossible.'

Lady Crale cleared her throat. 'You must excuse me for speaking frankly to you, Harriet. You are without mother and father. You have no guardian and therefore it is my Christian duty to take upon myself that responsibility whilst you are under my roof. I must now ask you a question of the utmost delicacy.' She paused awkwardly. 'On your journey to Khartoum, did Mr Beauvais display any untoward intimacy towards you?'

Harriet's cheeks flushed hotly.

Lady Crale passed a hand across her eyes. 'I see. It is worse than

I had feared.' She stood up and began to pace the room, saying agitatedly,

'There can be no question of reparation, Harriet. Mr Beauvais has treated you infamously. If you had hoped for marriage, I must disillusion you. The Beauvais are one of the oldest and richest families of France. The differences between your social positions are enormous: insurmountable. Under the circumstances there must be no delay in your returning to Cairo and home.' Her voice shook with emotion. 'His seduction of you is inexcusable. It is . . .'

Harriet sprang to her feet. 'Seduction? I have told you repeatedly that Mr Beauvais' behaviour towards me was that of a gentleman! He did not take advantage of me in the way that you are suggesting! Indeed, he was most careful of my reputation. He wanted me to be suitably chaperoned by you before announcing his intentions.'

Lady Crale's eyebrows rose. 'His intentions?'

'Yes . . . He . . .' Harriet floundered. 'He was going to ask for my hand in marriage.'

Lady Crale's face was incredulous. 'Mr Beauvais is a confirmed bachelor. Besides, I have explained to you that he is no ordinary gentleman. Why, he is a personal friend of the Emperor! I am afraid that he has been toying with your affections, Harriet. Possibly in the hope that such a promise would persuade you to become his mistress.'

'But I am not so!'

Lady Crale looked at the tormented young woman before her and knew that she spoke the truth. 'Then let us be grateful that your upbringing rendered you immune from his blandishments,' she said, walking towards Harriet and resting her hands on her shoulders. 'You have been sorely deceived, child. You are not the first. Others, more sophisticated than yourself, have also been taken in by Raoul Beauvais' smooth tongue and unscrupulous charm. I suggest that you sleep now. Your feeling of betrayal will have lessened by the morning.' She leaned forward and kissed Harriet briefly on the cheek before leaving the room.

Harriet covered her face with her hands, reliving every word and gesture that had passed between herself and Raoul Beauvais.

Had she assumed too much? A sliver of ice entered her heart. He had never told her he loved her. He had never said that he wished her to become his wife. She had thought the words unnecessary. She walked out on to the darkened balcony, her eyes anguished. He had kissed her and she had responded. She had built up a castle of dreams, believing herself to be loved and cherished. The first sign that she was not so had been his strange behaviour when they had arrived in Khartoum. His assertions that he had business that was more important than escorting her to the consulate. Had that business been his reunion with a dark-eyed, dusky-skinned slave who had aroused the interest of all Khartoum?

'No,' she whispered beneath her breath. 'No, no. It cannot be!' She remembered Berber and the Pasha's residence and the way he had introduced her in order to protect her reputation: as his cousin. For a few delirious moments she had thought, even then, that he was going to announce her as his bride-to-be. He had not done so. According to Lady Crale he would never do so.

There was a slight knock at the door and Jali entered.

'I have come to assist you with your gown,' she said shyly.

Mechanically Harriet turned and allowed Jali to undo the buttons of her gown. The rose-pink taffeta slid from her shoulders and she stepped out of the fine material without a backward glance.

'Lady Crale has asked me to give you a cooling powder,' Jali said, motioning to the glass that she had set on a low table. 'It will help you to sleep.'

'Thank you.'

Jali's eyes were troubled. She had overheard the conversation between her mistress and the English girl. She would have liked to have spoken to the English girl but it was not her place to do so and would only incur Lady Crale's wrath. Unhappily she left the room and as she closed the door behind her she heard the sound of bitter tears.

When Harriet awoke she lay for a few moments staring at the ceiling and the brilliant shafts of sunlight. Her head ached from the tears of the previous evening. She rose and drew back the shutters, immediately assailed by the sights and sounds of Africa. Why had she cried so? She hadn't believed the monstrous allegations made about Raoul. Today he would visit her at the consulate and there would be apologies from Lady Crale and her son. Later on there would be apologies from the Walthers also. Raoul had been away many weeks, possibly months, on his expedition and no doubt it had been in his absence that the vicious tongues had started to wag. She had never paid heed to gossip, not even when it had been the harmless gossip enjoyed by her aunts. Certainly she was not going to pay any heed to the dinner table gossip of the previous evening. Raoul was visiting her today. He would tell her the truth.

Lady Crale had been generous in her hospitality. Other gowns hung beside the rose-pink taffeta. Different gowns in light, cool muslin. Harriet hesitated and then dressed in the high-necked, full-sleeved and tight-wristed blouse that Hashim had procured for her in Berber. Both the blouse and the accompanying skirt had been scrupulously cleaned and ironed and though less fashionable than the ones that hung so enticingly in the vast wardrobe, they had come from Raoul and she valued them accordingly.

Jali entered shyly to assist her in her toilette, braiding Harriet's long golden hair with obvious pleasure.

Harriet watched her through the glass and wondered if the girl was an employed servant or a slave. Sebastian Crale had intimated that Europeans in Khartoum made use of slaves but that they did so circumspectly. It had been the openness of Raoul's buying of the Circassian that had caused outrage.

'Have you been in Lady Crale's service long, Jali?' she asked as the deft-fingered girl braided her hair.

'Many months,' Jali said with a smile. 'My brother is groom here and my aunt is in the kitchens.'

Harriet toyed with her glass-stoppered jar of rose-water. 'Does Lady Crale have slaves as the Turkish governors do?'

Jali shook her head vehemently. 'There are no slaves in her ladyship's household. Her ladyship thinks slavery is very bad . . . very wicked.'

'But other people keep slaves?' Harriet asked.

'Of course. There have always been slaves in Khartoum. It is better to be a slave than to starve.'

'Thank you, Jali.' Harriet rose to her feet. She had intended asking the servant girl if Raoul Beauvais kept slaves but could not bring herself to do so. She would discuss the subject with no one but Raoul himself. Not even with Lady Crale.

'My dear child, you look charming and perfectly refreshed,' Lady Crale said as Harriet entered the breakfast room. 'I have heard from my husband this morning. He expects to be in Khartoum by the end of the month. I think we can safely leave arrangements for your return to England in his hands.'

Despite the heat, silver salvers held bacon, kidneys, scrambled eggs and kedgeree. Harriet ignored them and contented herself with coffee and fresh fruit.

'Dr Walther was most concerned about your health last evening. I assured him that it was merely tiredness but he insisted on seeing you. Rather than him calling here, I thought it would be more enjoyable for you if we visited him. The carriage ride will give you an opportunity to see more of the city and I like to pay my calls in the morning. After midday the heat makes any kind of exercise impossible.'

'Oh, but . . .' Harriet protested and then halted. A refusal to go because of Raoul Beauvais' expected visit would only reopen the distressing conversation of the previous evening.

'Sebastian will be accompanying us. He and Dr Walther are to be companions on an expedition in the near future and are both making plans.'

Harriet curbed her initial panic. The visit was to be a morning one and no doubt they would have returned before Raoul called at the consulate. Even if they had not done so, he would call later in the day and the very fact that a message would have been left would prepare Lady Crale for the apology she would have to make.

Sebastian Crale entered and served himself generously with eggs and bacon.

'You gave us all a fright last evening, Miss Latimer. I am glad to see that you are looking as ravishing as ever this morning.'

Lady Crale frowned and tapped her foot impatiently on the floor. At twenty-seven, Sebastian's romantic entanglements had all been undesirable and he was going to make an already complicated situation worse if he persisted in paying such attention to Henry Latimer's penniless daughter. She had not been happy at his proposed trek south, but now she viewed it with a certain amount of relief. The expedition left within days. It would curtail any involvement Sebastian might be contemplating where Harriet was concerned.

'We are leaving for the Walther's at ten o'clock, Sebastian. Please be ready or I shall be obliged to leave without you.' Her tone of voice made her displeasure at his behaviour obvious. Sebastian was unrepentant and annoyingly on time.

The open carriage was lavishly sprung, and if she had been in the streets of Cheltenham Harriet would have considered herself to be in the lap of luxury. The noise and smell of Khartoum overcame any such pleasures. Narrow, dusty streets teemed with natives and traders. Now and then there was a glimpse of the Nile and a litter of masts and felucca sails. Close to, the mosques were shabby, their domes and minarets tawdry. Harriet lowered her veil to shield her face from the dust and flies. Lady Crale was pointing out to her the governor's palace and other landmarks which she thought might be of interest. Harriet smiled politely and murmured appropriate remarks, but her thoughts were elsewhere: with Raoul and whether or not he was already at the consulate and annoyed at finding her absent. They had been apart for a day. Every hour seemed a lifetime. She had never imagined it possible to miss any human being so much. She ached for his company; for his deep, strong voice; for his laughter and even for his anger. Sebastian Crale sat inches away from her and she found his presence an irritation. She wanted to see dark eyes in a hawklike face, not grey eyes and sleek moustaches. She wanted to see the lean, tanned contours of a body used to decisive action, not the softness of a man accustomed to being driven in a carriage. She yearned for the indefinable smell of maleness and not the sweet perfume of Sebastian Crale's eau de cologne.

She wanted reassurance: she wanted to be told that the stories bandied about the Crale's dinner table had been scandalous lies. She wanted to hear him ask formally for her hand in marriage. She felt hot, remembering his kisses, his touch. She wanted him and him only for the rest of her life.

Lady Crale tapped an ivory-topped cane on the carriage floor in exasperation. 'How foolish of the man to have taken this route! He should have avoided the square at all costs! It will be near half an hour before we are free of this mob!'

Waking from her private reverie, Harriet looked around her with surprise. The carriage was at a near standstill, the crowds were so thick. A little way in front of them was a square and it was obviously the driver's intention to cross it. It also seemed to be the sole destination of the crowds around them.

'What is the attraction?' Harriet asked curiously.

'A slave auction,' Lady Crale said, tight-lipped. 'How the Turks can deny such things exist when they take place for all to see, I cannot imagine.'

The noise and the clamour had intensified and then, by dint of brute force and little regard for those underfoot, the horses broke through and Lady Crale's carriage hurtled out of the street and into the square. Harriet gasped and the colour left her face.

'It's as well for you to see for yourself,' Lady Crale said, averting her eyes. 'Unless you do, you will never be able to conceive the barbarity of the slavers.'

They stood on the auction block, men, women and children yoked together like cattle. Half dead from hunger, naked and bewildered, they ranged in a long line from the youngest to the oldest.

Lady Crale urged the driver to make a speedy exit from the foetid square, as embarrassed by the nakedness of the women on public display as she was at their being displayed at all. Harriet tried to avert her head and could not. The slaves' eyes were dull and listless. The eyes of those who had long since abandoned all hope, their bodies covered in sores and whip marks. At either end of the chained line guards with swords and spears stood to attention while the slave traders prodded first one and then another.

'What is he saying?' Harriet asked, her voice a whisper of horror.

Lady Crale did not hear her. She was too busy exhorting the carriage driver to remove them from the scene.

Sebastian Crale looked uncomfortable. 'He is telling prospective buyers what tribes his slaves are from. The light-coloured, bearded slaves are probably Nyam-Nyam from the south-west and cannibals. The black fellows Madis; the thin-legged slaves Dinkas or Shiluks. The handsome fellow at the end is probably a Calas or a Bonga and the undersized ones are the Akka pygmies.'

Harriet pressed a handkerchief against her mouth as several of the girls were made to walk and run for the benefit of prospective buyers.

Sebastian Crale shifted uneasily on the leather-padded seat of the carriage. 'It is unfortunate that you have had to see this, Miss Latimer. Usually they hold their auctions in the desert on the outskirts of the city. The bought slaves are then marched off along caravan routes to the Red Sea for shipment to Arabia or Persia. This particular trader would not have had the effrontery to have held this auction here if my father had been in the city.'

'Can't we stop it?' Harriet asked in anguish. 'Is there nothing we can do?'

Sebastian looked perplexed. 'Against this crowd?'

Harriet was uncaring of the crowd. She cried out in protest as a crying woman was released from the chains and handed to an Arab for a paltry number of notes.

Lady Crale's head swivelled. Sebastian Crale blinked. Harriet was uncaring. 'We can't just watch and drive on while people are being sold like beasts!'

'Contain yourself, Harriet,' Lady Crale said firmly as heads began to turn in their direction. 'There is nothing we can do.' She smacked the driver on the shoulder with her cane. 'I demand we leave this square *immediately!*'

'He won't do so well with that lot,' Sebastian remarked as the carriage finally shot out of the square. 'The slaves who bring high prices are the Abyssinian and Circassian girls bought for the harems of the East.' Harriet shuddered. No wonder her father had devoted his whole life to fighting against such barbarity.

She was so distressed that she took very little part in the conversation at the Walther's. Magdalene was chillingly polite, reserving all her friendliness for Sebastian. Dr Walther was genuinely concerned for her health and when assured by Lady Crale that she was quite recovered, beamed thankfully and didn't persist in his questioning.

'We shall be leaving within days,' he was saying to Lady Crale, polishing his glasses furiously. 'The expedition to end all expeditions!'

'The hunting will be phenomenal,' Sebastian added, his eyes lighting up with enthusiasm. 'Rhino and hippos and elephants in plenty.'

'And fame,' Magdalene added, her dark-lidded eyes burning with sudden passion.

Harriet tried to pay attention. She had lost the drift of the conversation going on around her.

'I would be surprised if you managed to journey further south than Gondokoro, Dr Walther,' Lady Crale said, balancing a china teacup and saucer delicately in a white-gloved hand.

'Nonsense!' Dr Walther said good humouredly, striding backwards and forwards, his hands clasped behind his back. 'We are well equipped and able. This time the question of the Nile will finally be resolved! We shall find out the truth, Lady Crale. The Nile's source will be a secret no longer!' His eyes had the same glazed expression in them that Harriet had often seen in her father's.

'Is that the purpose of your expedition?' she asked, gazing at Sebastian and Dr Walther incredulously. 'To find the source of the Nile?'

'It is!' Dr Walther's cherubic face was ecstatic. 'I have spent a whole year planning, six months preparing. We are waiting for one gentleman only and he is now amongst us.'

Lady Crale coughed. Dr Walther looked suitable chastened.

'A necessity, Lady Crale,' he murmured. 'We cannot choose our companions in such circumstances. We must journey with those best suited to our purpose.'

Harriet set her cup and saucer down on a chinese lacquered table. 'I hope you are successful,' she said quietly. 'It was my father's dream to find the secret source of the Nile.'

Lady Crale rose to her feet. She had no intention of discussing such inanities any further. The expedition would reach Gondokoro, the farthest point south that was mapped, and would return. It would keep Sebastian out of trouble for six months and enable her to come to an arrangement with a bosom friend. The friend has a daughter who, at twenty-one, was not yet married, nor seemed likely to be. Sebastian could be coerced. There would be a wedding before the year was out if she had to drag her son to the altar herself.

'You are leaving so soon?' Dr Walther asked, disappointment flooding his face.

'Sebastian is staying. I understand there are still things to discuss in connection with your expedition. Good day, Mr Walther. Good day, Magdalene.'

Magdalene, happily unaware of Lady Crale's plans for a suitable bride for Sebastian, was almost pleasant as they took their leave.

Harriet smiled at her warmly, overjoyed at the prospect of an early return to the consulate. He would be there. He would be waiting for her. His dark eyes would be angry, his sun-bronzed face hard and uncompromising. Then she would tell him of how she had been obliged to accompany Lady Crale to the Walther's and the hard lines of his mouth would soften. He would ask for permission to speak to her alone and Lady Crale would be baffled and disconcerted, but would have to grant him his request. He would take her in his arms, kissing her with unsuppressed passion and she would yield as naturally as a flower opening its petals to the sun. He would ask her to be his wife and together they would face Lady Crale and all misunderstandings would be a thing of the past.

'Raoul,' she said softly to herself. 'Raoul . . .'

He was there, head and shoulders above the crowd, sleek black hair gleaming in the sun, curling low in the nape of his neck, his strong-boned face instantly distinctive amongst the surge of Arabs and Turks who thronged around him. Her heart seemed to cease beating. For a second she could not breathe and then joy welled up in her like a shining fountain. 'Raoul!' she called, ignoring Lady Crale's gasps of horror. '*Raoul!*'

He was striding quickly through the crowd, talking to a companion that Harriet could not see.

'Raoul!' She rose in the moving carriage, waving frantically. The crowd surged and fleetingly parted.

The girl at his side was no older than herself. Olive skin glistened seductively. Ebony hair hung sleekly down her back. Her robe shimmered, fluttering round her slender body. Smooth, neat feet were sandalled as Harriet's had been on the journey from Berber. They were walking quickly and as a portly gentleman threatened to separate them, she saw Raoul's hand reach out and grasp the girl's wrist. He was looking down at her, his face animated.

The girl said something and Harriet saw him laugh, and then they continued, threading their way deftly through the crowd, oblivious of Lady Crale's carriage. Oblivious of Harriet's stricken figure.

'This sort of behaviour will not do ... Most unsuitable ... A disgraceful exhibition for a young lady of your upbringing ...' Lady Crale's words were lost on Harriet.

She stared sightlessly, seeing only a sun-bronzed hand grasping a darker one. She had shut out the truth, clinging to her dreams. Now she could cling to them no longer. He had never said he loved her because he had not done so. He had amused himself with her. No doubt she had been a welcome diversion on the tedious journey to Khartoum. She remembered how easily she had submitted to his kisses and caresses, and her cheeks burned. She had forfeited respect and dignity to a man who bought slaves to satisfy his lust. A man no different from the Pasha. She fought back humiliating tears. She had believed him honourable and brave. She had given him her heart freely and joyfully and now she was bereft. Raoul did not love her: had never loved her. It seemed a thing too monstrous to be true.

Lady Crale was still shaking with anger as they were helped from the carriage.

'To call out in the street ... after all that has been said ... To draw attention to yourself in such a manner ...'

Harriet was barely aware of her. Lost in her own private hell she walked up the broad sweep of stairs and closed the door of her room behind her. Jali knocked timidly and was ignored. The sun was at its highest: the low ceilinged room like a furnace. Mechanically she closed the shutters, plunging the room into shadow. She had given her heart, now she must retrieve it. She lay down on the bed and two large tears eased their way from beneath her eyelids and coursed slowly down her cheeks. She had been rash and foolish and unwise. Something cold and hard settled deep within her. She would not be so again. If love brought such pain then she would live without it.

Chapter Six

The hammering on the door of the consulate aroused Harriet from her stupor. She lay for a moment, listening intently, and then panic gripped her. There could be no mistaking that voice. Faithless, straight from the arms of another woman, he had come as he said he would. Her heart beat wildly as she ran to the door and opened it, listening more clearly to the angry words that were now floating up from Lady Crale's marbled-floored hallway. He had gained entry, probably by brute force. Lady Crale's voice was high-pitched with outrage, Raoul's tightly controlled but throbbing with suppressed rage.

'I shall contaminate the British consulate for as long as it takes me to speak with Miss Latimer!'

'You shall not do so! Miss Latimer is under my charge and is indisposed.'

'She is sick?' The words were like a whiplash.

'Yes . . . No . . . She is indisposed . . .' Lady Crale's authority was fast deserting her.

'Then I must and will see her!'

There was the sound of booted feet striding to the foot of the stairs. Lady Crale's voice rose hysterically. Servants were summoned and Lady Crale demanded they evict Mr Beauvais forcibly. There was no sound of anyone attempting to do so. He was taking the stairs two at a time. Harriet pressed her hand against her pulsating heart and stepped outside the door, standing motionless.

He halted, one hand on the banisters, looking up at her. The anxiety that had been on his face vanished. White teeth flashed in a broad smile, his eyes full of laughter. She could see tiny flecks of gold near the dark pupils.

'Lady Crale is a more than adequate chaperon,' he said, not closing the distance between them but surveying her with pleasure. 'I've had the devil of a job to get this far.'

The strong sunlight had been behind her, casting her pale hair into a golden nebula and showing only the slender outline of her figure. Now she moved forward fractionally and his smile vanished. There was no welcome on her face: it was a frozen mask. The green-gold eyes those of a stranger.

'There was no need for such dramatics,' she said coldly, striving to keep her voice steady, wishing that he would look away from her, that he would step backwards and so increase the distance between them.

'I wished to see you.' It was a flat statement. The laughter and the smiles had vanished.

'It was kind of you to call, Mr Beauvais,' she said formally, betraying none of her inner tumult. 'I would like to thank you for escorting me to Khartoum.' She gave a stiff, dismissive smile. 'And now, if you will excuse me, I must rest. I find the heat of the afternoon overpowering.'

She turned swiftly, aware that anguished tears were threatening to spill down her cheeks.

His eyes blazed. In swift strides he mounted the stairs between them and grasped hold of her wrist.

With violent fury she wrenched herself free, the imprint of another hand so held burning in her memory like fire.

'Don't touch me!' she cried passionately. 'Don't ever touch me again!'

If she had struck him he could not have looked more stunned.

'Harriet, for God's sake!'

The door slammed in his face.

'Harriet!' He beat on it with his fists.

Harriet leaned on the far side, her head thrown back, her eyes closed, tears falling unrestrainedly.

'Harriet! *Harriet!*'

There came the sound of other feet running up the stairs; of shouts and altercations and then a bitter oath as Raoul swung on his heels and marched in blazing fury to where Lady Crale waited for him.

Lady Crale had had time to compose herself. 'You demanded to see Miss Latimer. You have seen her. I would now be obliged if you would leave the consulate immediately.'

'It will be a pleasure,' he said savagely. 'But before I do I want to know what has been said to Miss Latimer in the twenty-four hours she has been beneath this roof.'

Lady Crale raised her eyebrows archly. 'Said? She has been welcomed; given shelter . . .'

The lines around his mouth were white. 'You know very well to what I refer. I parted with Miss Latimer yesterday on friendly terms. Now she refuses to speak to me.'

'There is no cause for you to do so. You have ascertained that she arrived here safely. She has thanked you for your protection and now the matter is at an end.'

'Afternoon, Beauvais,' Sebastian said genially, walking in on them, impervious to the highly-charged atmosphere. 'Walther tells me we are ready to leave within days.' He gestured towards a round-eyed servant. 'Take this to Miss Latimer with my compliments.' He pointed towards a hatbox elaborately trimmed. 'I had a devil of a job hunting this down. Khartoum does not abound in milliners.'

'Circumstances,' Lady Crale continued, her eyes holding Raoul's unflinchingly, 'change, Mr Beauvais. I am sure you understand.'

Raoul's eyes flashed from Sebastian Crale to the hatbox and back again. 'I understand perfectly,' he rasped and stormed towards the door, obliging Sebastian to step back quickly to avoid being knocked aside.

He had barely recovered his balance when his mother swung round on him. 'Miss Latimer is a missionary's daughter. You will oblige me by treating her as such. The gift of a hat is totally inappropriate.'

She swept past him towards the consul's study. The situation had become impossible. Christian duty had been done and could be carried no further. Amongst Khartoum's residents, there must be someone travelling to Cairo. Someone who could escort Miss Harriet Latimer far away from the British consulate. Away from Raoul Beauvais and his insufferable rudeness; away from her son and his dangerous infatuation.

Harriet was still trembling so violently that she had to clasp her hands in her lap as Lady Crale stood imposingly before her. She had intended to vent her wrath on Harriet. After all, neither of the disgraceful scenes in the market place or the consulate would have taken place if it hadn't been for Harriet's presence. However, the small white face with the large tragic eyes softened her heart. The girl had behaved foolishly but she had also suffered. First the hideous death of her father and then the misfortune of being rescued by a man who was a notorious breaker of hearts.

She said quietly, 'I think you will agree with me that it would be best for you to leave for Cairo at the earliest opportunity.'

Harriet nodded dumbly.

'There are only thirty Europeans at present in Khartoum but I shall find out, within the next few days, which, if any, are returning to Cairo. Failing that, we must await my husband and he will no doubt instruct his aide to escort you.'

'Thank you.' Harriet's voice was low, thick with suppressed tears.

Lady Crale said compassionately, 'You have seen for yourself that Mr Beauvais' behaviour is not that of a gentleman. I pray that you will put all thoughts of him from your mind. No doubt you will soon find yourself married on your return to England. A clergyman perhaps . . .'

Harriet thought of the Reverend March-Allinson and shook her head, her pain so intense she had to stop herself from crying out.

Lady Crale, mistaking her silence for acceptance, breathed a sigh of relief and left the room. She would approach Hubert Pennyfax. As a big game hunter, he regularly made the arduous journey to the coast with ivory and live specimens for European menageries.

Harriet walked slowly out on to the balcony. In the distance the White and Blue Niles merged and flowed southward a mile wide. Her father had hoped to discover its source. Dr Walther and

Sebastian Crale were journeying on the same mission. She longed to join them. The doctor and Sebastian did not have to return to a claustrophobic existence in England. Men – they could do as they pleased. Her head throbbed. The rage she had felt when Raoul had grasped her wrist as he had his slave girl's, had been replaced by sweeping desolation. Beyond the city the desert stretched in hot silence. Once it had been her enemy but now she felt irrevocably drawn to it and to what lay beyond. To the Africa of mystery and legend.

She could not stay in Khartoum. Her behaviour had offended Lady Crale and although she had spoken to her with remarkable kindness, Harriet knew that their relationship had been irreparably strained. Within weeks, possibly days, she would be accompanied to Cairo and then undertake the long journey to England and Cheltenham. She could not return to such an existence. Not now; not after experiencng the dangers and excitement of a continent barely explored.

She stood for so long that dusk began to fall. She did not have to return to England. Lady Crale was not her legal guardian and could not oblige her to do so. She could do what she had intended to do all along. She could continue southwards into unknown country and discover the fabled fountains of the Nile. Only her companions would be Dr Walther and Sebastian Crale, and not her dearly loved father.

Her determination increased. Her broken heart could not be mended by returning to England and marrying the kind of man Lady Crale would consider suitable. Her heart had been given once. It could not be given again. But the pain it held could be eased. Danger would surely erase the tortured memories of Raoul Beauvais from her mind. She turned, pacing the room, her mind racing furiously. Lady Crale would be aghast, but she was not Lady Crale's charge. Her life was her own, to do with as she pleased. There would be no return to Cheltenham with its green lawns and sweet-scented roses. Instead she would journey south to the snow-capped fields of Kilimanjaro. She dined alone in her room, much to Sebastian's disappointment. The next day she expressed a desire to see the Walthers again and Lady Crale, assuming that Harriet wished to renew her acquaintance with Magdalene, readily agreed.

'My dear Miss Latimer, what a delightful surprise! A glass of sherry? Lime juice? Dates?'

Servants hurried around, proffering drinks and dainties as Mr Walther ushered her into his over-furnished rooms.

'A glass of lime juice, please,' Harriet said, glad to see that Magdalene was absent.

Dr Walther removed a sextant and a barometer from a chair, enabling Harriet to take a seat.

'We have so little time,' he said as he removed a telescope and a chronometer from another chair and sat down. 'Our expedition leaves on Friday. Just think of it, Miss Latimer! After a year of planning, at last we are to set sail!'

'It is your expedition that I wish to discuss,' Harriet said, sipping her drink.

Dr Walther's moon face beamed with pleasure. 'It will establish me as the greatest explorer of the century,' he said, innocently repeating words Harriet had heard her father speak. 'Here is the map.' He pushed bits of paper to one side and spread a large map out on the table. 'Here is Khartoum,' a stubby finger jabbed at the point where two thin blue lines met. 'Here is Gondokoro.' His finger travelled southwards. 'That is the furthest point south that has been travelled in the many attempts to find the source of the Nile.' He took off his spectacles and began to polish them vigorously. 'Beyond Gondokoro the Niles races through rapids barring any further advance.'

'Yet you intend to travel further?'

'Oh, yes. Yes. We are taking oxen and mules. We shall travel by land until the river is once more navigable.'

'Is there a town at Gondokoro?' Harriet asked curiously.

Dr Walther shook his head. 'Some years ago Austrian priests established a mission there, but they died of sickness. I doubt if they made a single convert. Some slavers sail that far south – the more reckless and adventurous ones. Otherwise it is nothing but a name and one that is known to only a handful of people. It is beyond civilisation and I have never yet met any man who has travelled there and returned.'

'My father knew nothing of Gondokoro. Khartoum was the furthest point south on his map. Nevertheless, he intended obtaining supplies here and following the river wherever it led. To find the Nile's source was his dearest dream.'

Dr Walther sighed rapturously. 'For centuries it has been the dream of many men. I, Franz Walther, am going to make that dream a reality.'

Harriet said carefully, 'It was my intention to accompany my father.'

Dr Walther blinked uncomprehendingly.

Harriet took a deep breath. 'The dream was not my father's alone. It was also mine. I still wish to fulfil it. I would dearly like to be included in your expedition, Dr Walther.'

'I am afraid you have misunderstood, Miss Latimer. Our expedition will face great hardships. Unimaginable difficulties . . .'

'I survived the Nubian Desert, Dr Walther,' Harriet said spiritedly. 'I am well aware of the kind of difficulties you envisage.'

'But our expeditionary leader would not allow it. He is adamant that only qualified scientists and geographers are to be among our party.'

'Is Sebastian Crale a scientist or geographer?' Harriet asked, surprised.

Dr Walther looked flustered. 'Sebastian is a special case.'

'In what way?'

'His father is the consul here. There would have been difficulties if we had not included him in our party.'

'So exceptions *have* been made?'

'Only one, Miss Latimer. I do assure you, most warmly, that the expedition will not be the romance you imagine.'

'I do not expect it to be romantic at all.' Harriet's voice held a note of sharpness. She had no desire to be reminded of romance. 'Have you a nurse in your party?'

'No . . .'

'Then I will fill that capacity. I am also a more than adequate artist. No doubt the geographical societies will appreciate detailed drawings of the flora and fauna of the upper banks of the Nile. I think I will be quite a useful addition to your party, Dr Walther.'

'But Miss Latimer!' Dr Walther's distress was pathetic. 'We are a party of *men*. It is impossible . . .'

'Do not worry on that score,' Harriet said bleakly. 'I am not looking for a husband. Only adventure.' She rose to her feet. 'I shall be ready to leave on Friday, Dr Walther.'

'I cannot give that permission! I am not the expedition's leader. It is for him to say if you can join us or not.'

'Then you must give me his name and tell me where I can find him.'

'His name,' a hard voice said from some feet behind her, 'is Beauvais. And you'll find him here, Miss Latimer.'

Harriet swirled around, the blood draining from her face.

He was leaning against the open door, his eyes black pits in which she could read nothing. He moved forward into the room, pouring himself a small measure of brandy from Dr Walther's decanter, his manner as insolently self-assured as it had been in the Pasha's residence.

'You wished to ask me something, I believe?' he said lazily, sitting on the edge of a mahogany table, one leg swinging free, swirling the brandy around in the glass. His expressionless eyes studied her face. Which was the real Harriet? The one he had held in his arms in the lone desert, or the outraged female proclaiming to the world that her virtue was beyond reproach? That nothing had passed between them. That she held him in the same regard as the rest of her narrow-minded, prim and proper country-women.

Harriet fought for breath and control. If she abandoned her dream because of Raoul Beauvais he would have gained yet another victory over her, and he would know it. Her heart pounded with physical pain.

'You no doubt overheard my conversation with Dr Walther,' she said tersely, 'and know very well what it is that I wish to ask.'

Her eyes as they met his were contemptuous. Raoul downed the brandy. The laughing, unconventional, delightful girl of the desert had disappeared. She had been occasioned only by circumstance. This was the real Miss Latimer. No different from her contemporaries: the kind of girl who put so-called respectability above any feelings of the heart. His eyes raked her slowly, from head to toe, so that she felt naked before his gaze and then he said tauntingly,

'But I wish you to ask it, Miss Latimer.'

Harriet threw her head back defiantly, her eyes blazing. Damn him, but he would not have the satisfaction of seeing her turn tail. Eyes blazing, she said with such viciousness that Dr Walther shrank back against the wall,

'I wish to join the expedition south in search of the Nile's source. You have no nurse. I can nurse. You have no artist to record flora and fauna. I can draw.'

'And are those your only credentials?' The corner of his mouth lifted in a smile as though he were amused.

She felt a flash of white-hot rage. 'It is enough!'

His eyes held hers and this time there was an expression in them that sent desire flooding through her so that she felt shameless. She clenched her fists, hating herself for the knowledge that she was as much in love with him as ever.

'And what of your companions, Miss Latimer?' he asked, with a depth of feeling that startled the doctor even further. 'Are they not part of the reason you wish to make the journey?'

Her throat felt tight. She could hardly speak the words. 'Dr Walther and Sebastian Crale I barely know. The other members of your party I know not at all. As for yourself, I would be more than happy never to set eyes on you again!'

'Then rest assured, madam, that you will not.' He slid to his feet and replenished his glass. 'No woman accompanies us: least of all yourself. Good day, Miss Latimer.'

Tears of anger and frustration stung her eyes. She choked them back. She would *not* beg or plead: she would *not* allow him to see the depth of her disappointment. She marched towards the door, her head high.

'Good day, Dr Walther. I hope we meet again in happier circumstances.'

She threw a withering look in Raoul Beauvais' direction, but it was lost on him. He merely shrugged and a mirthless smile tinged the hard lines of his mouth.

Not until she regained her own room at the consulate did she stop shaking. How dare he suggest that she wanted to join the expedition in order to continue a liaison with him! Had her behaviour on the journey to Khartoum been so low and unseemly? She thought of the burning kisses given and accepted freely and her cheeks flamed with shame. She should have known from the outset that a man like Raoul Beauvais would not be the kind of man to live alone: that there would be a wife or mistress waiting for him on his return. She splashed her face with cool water, attempting to regain her composure. She had envisaged neither. Certainly she had not envisaged a slave girl enjoying the same embraces that she had cherished so dearly. She patted her face dry and looked at herself in the mirror above the wash stand. Eyes filled with misery seemed huge in her whitened face. In the brief moments in Khartoum's square she had seen what Lady Crale had not. She had seen the expression in the Circassian's eyes as Raoul had grasped her wrist. They had held the same expression that had once been in her own. Bought or not, Raoul Beauvais' slave girl was as much in love with him as she herself. And he was faithful to neither of them. Desolation swept over her. She had probably set eyes on him for the last time. Soon, Africa too, would be nothing but a memory. She would live sedately in Cheltenham, the uneventful years slipping by until at last she was as old and fixed in her ways as her aunts.

'Damn!' she cried explosively, throwing herself on to the bed and pummelling the pillows, giving vent to the tears she had been suppressing. 'Damn, damn, damn!'

Lady Crale was disturbed to discover that her son was dining with them once again. Generally he dined alone or with friends. Some suitable, as in the case of Dr Walther: some unsuitable, as in the case of the unspeakable Mr Beauvais. That he should dine at the consulate when no other guests were invited could only mean that the attraction was Harriet. Lady Crale picked listlessly at her food. When she had agreed to offer hospitality to Harriet Latimer she had never imagined that the girl would be a natural beauty, capable of turning heads in the capitals of Europe, let alone a forsaken outpost like Khartoum. She had expected a missionary's daughter to look like a missionary's daughter. Harriet Latimer did not. Nor did she behave like one.

She signalled for the servants to bring in the fish course. Harriet Latimer's outburst at Raoul Beauvais when he had stormed the consulate had been correct in that she had shown no desire to encourage his attentions, but it had shown a passionate intensity that was disturbing. Polite and well-mannered though she was, Lady Crale judged Harriet to be an unknown quantity and one that was best kept far away from her son. She shuddered involuntarily. After all these years of bachelorhood, if Sebastian should marry a missionary's daughter, she would never be able to hold her head high in London society again.

'The natives say the Nile springs from great inland lakes,' Sebastian was saying enthusiastically to a strained-looking Harriet. 'The Great Nyanzas, they call them.'

'I am tired of hearing about the source of that wretched river,' Lady Crale said with unexpected asperity. 'It is all you have discussed for six months. Who cares where it springs from?'

'The whole of Europe,' Sebastian said disarmingly.

'The whole of Europe should try living out here,' Lady Crale said tartly. 'They would soon lose interest in everything African.'

She turned to Harriet. The bloom that had been on the girl's cheeks had faded, her flawless skin was pale, her green-gold eyes bleak. Instead of detracting from her beauty, her distress enhanced it. Lady Crale was well aware of the effect it was having on her son. He was feeling protective as well as beguiled. It was a potent combination and one that filled her with dismay.

'You will be pleased to hear, Harriet, that I have been able to make arrangements for you to return to Cairo with all speed. Mr and Mrs Pennyfax are returning early next week. Mr Pennyfax is something of an eccentric. He has already travelled extensively in South America and the East. Mrs Pennyfax is quite an indomitable traveller herself and will be an ideal chaperon. I think I can promise that your return journey will not be the nightmare your outward journey proved to be. They travel with a large contingent of servants and you will enjoy as much comfort as is possible in the circumstances.'

'Thank you.' Harriet smiled, but the corners of her lips trembled. Sebastian Crale wondered what it would be like to kiss that soft-looking mouth. The girl did not want to return to England. She wanted to remain in Khartoum and he believed he knew why. Nothing had been said between them, but he had made his feelings obvious by the tone of his voice and the expression in his eyes. Harriet Latimer wanted to remain at the consulate until he returned. The most curious longing swept through him. It would be an exceedingly pleasant sensation to have the golden-haired Miss Latimer waiting in Khartoum for his return from the interior.

'I do not think it is necessary for Miss Latimer to return to Cairo with the Penny-faxes,' he said, smoothing his immaculate moustache with his forefinger, his eyes riveted on Harriet's slender figure. 'I think it would be more suitable if she remained in Khartoum for a while. She needs a longer period of rest before embarking on the journey back.'

'Allow me to know what is best,' his mother said icily, glaring at him down the length of the silver-laden table. 'The Penny-faxes leave next week and so does Miss Latimer.'

Harriet regarded Lady Crale with puzzled and hurt eyes. The warmth that Lady Crale had displayed on welcoming her had virtually disappeared. Had her behaviour at calling out in public to Raoul Beauvais been so reprehensible? She pushed her plate away, the food untouched. She had her own answer. He had been openly consorting with a bought slave, flaunting the intimacy that existed between them. She felt so dispirited that she wondered if she was falling ill of some tropical fever. She raised a hand to her throbbing temple.

'Would you excuse me Lady Crale? I have a headache.'

Lady Crale nodded, excusing her with pleasure, grateful that her son was soon leaving on his expedition and that Harriet would shortly be travelling north. Another week of Miss Latimer's presence and Sebastian would be on the point of proposing marriage. She rose from the table. She was worrying unnecessarily. Sebastian would continue with his foolhardy expedition. He would return disillusioned and would marry a girl of her choice.

Sebastian sat for a long time over his port. If he didn't marry soon, he would find himself obliged to marry a girl of his mother's choice or have his income withdrawn. He could do far worse than marry Harriet Latimer. She would be far warmer in bed than any female of his mother's choosing. Musingly he drained his glass and climbed the shallow flight of stairs to his room.

When he asked her the next day if she would like to ride with him, Harriet accepted gratefully. The consulate had become claustrophobic. Friendliness on Lady Crale's part had been withdrawn: only formal politeness remained.

'The sun does not seem to affect you,' he said as they cantered out of the courtyard and into the hot, dusty streets.

'I have grown accustomed to it.'

'Then you are a rarity. Few men ever do so.'

It was still early and the city was not as crowded as it had been when she had made her fateful carriage ride.

'I was born in Egypt; perhaps that accounts for my adaptability.'

A smile curved his lips. 'That is another mystery less. How many more mysteries do you possess, Miss Latimer?'

With a shock Harriet realised that Sebastian Crale was flirting with her. She said politely, 'None,' and flicked her horse so that it moved a little further away from his mount.

'Miss Latimer.' His voice had changed. It was no longer bantering but full of emotion. 'I know that you do not wish to leave the city and I believe I know the reason why.'

She felt herself pale. 'You are mistaken, Mr Crale. I am more than ready to leave Khartoum at the first opportunity.'

He saw that her hand trembled slightly on the reins.

'Miss Latimer, I . . .'

'Are we forced to continue this way?' Harriet's voice rose in alarm. In front of them lay the river and a tangle of dhows and felucca sails.

'Dr Walther is supervising the loading of the boats this morning.'

Vainly Harriet looked around for a way of escape but Sebastian Crale was already slipping from his saddle and saying,

'We shall be away for at least a year and even for such a small party shall be taking three boats. This one will take the foodstuffs. The sacks the boys are carrying aboard now are full of grain.'

He held his hand out to help her dismount.

'I would rather not. I . . .'

It was too late. Dr Walther had already seen her and was hurrying across to them.

'Good morning, Miss Latimer! What a delightful surprise! I hope you have recovered from your disappointment.'

'Disappointment?' Sebastian Crale looked from the rotund little doctor to Harriet. 'What disappointment?'

Dr Walther's voice was compassionate. 'Miss Latimer had hoped to accompany us on our expedition, but Mr Beauvais has refused her permission to do so.'

Sebastian Crale looked down at Harriet incredulously. 'Is that true? Would you have gone to such lengths?'

Harriet refused to meet his eyes, grateful for the veiling on her broad-brimmed hat.

'I have no desire to discuss it,' she said tightly, the tears welling unbidden in her eyes.

Sebastian Crale took hold of her hands, imprisoning them in his.

'Miss Latimer,' he said, 'will you do me the honour of becoming my wife?' and before Harriet could recover from her stupefying amazement, he lifted her veil and, taking her in his arms, kissed her full on the mouth.

'A dockside is a strange choice for love-making,' a familiar deep voice said harshly.

Sebastian released a stunned Harriet and turned, angry spots of colour in his cheeks.

'What the devil is it to you, Beauvais?'

'Nothing,' Raoul said, his eyes brilliant pin-pricks in a face suddenly brutal, 'except that I have over ten tons of grain to load on to this boat and you and your inamorata are making the task impossible.'

Sebastian Crale's voice shook with rage. 'Apologise for that remark at once, Beauvais. You are speaking of my future wife.'

Raoul's eyes flickered from the outraged Sebastian, to where Harriet stood, her hand pressed against her pounding heart, her face devoid of colour.

'My felicitations. You make a most charming couple.'

'Thank you,' Sebastian said stiffly. 'Will the grain be loaded today?'

Raoul's reply was lost on Harriet. She was aware only of his sarcasm; of the contempt in his eyes and of a blazing anger that she could not understand. Aware that another second of his scrutiny would break her self-control altogether, she whirled around and marched to her horse, mounting despite Sebastian's shout of protest.

Furiously she dug her heels in the horse's flanks. What *right* had he to look at her in such a way? It was *his* behaviour that was at fault, not hers. *He* was the one who had returned to Khartoum and his mistress's caresses. If he had been a man of any honour he would have severed the connection immediately. But he was not a man of honour; the whole of Khartoum knew and talked of it, even those who were to be his companions.

She disregarded Sebastian Crale's shouts that she rein in and allow him to catch up with her. Because of Raoul Beauvais she would have to leave Africa. No other course of action was open to her: unless she married Sebastian Crale.

The idea was so amazing that she gasped. Had he really proposed to her only minutes ago? And if so, why? She had given him no encouragement, no indication that such a proposal would be welcome. Sebastian Crale was handsome, debonair, exquisitely mannered and no doubt heir to a fortune. However, he did not make her heart beat faster or her nerves throb as the detestable Raoul Beauvais did. His kiss had been remarkable only for its unexpectedness. Every kiss of Raoul's had seared her very soul. There could be no marriage to Sebastian Crale: no marriage to anyone. She was destined to become an old maid, living in Cheltenham, talking about bonnets and gowns and nursing a consuming jealousy for a girl bought on the auction block as a slave.

Chapter Seven

Sebastian galloped into the courtyard as Harriet dismounted. Panting for breath he slid from his horse and strode across to her.

'I hadn't realised Beauvais' words had distressed you so much. The man meant nothing by them. His manner is naturally abusive.'

'*That*,' Harriet said, struggling for control, 'I well know!'

Sebastian frowned. He had not been aware that Harriet was acquainted with Beauvais. He cast it from his mind. He had other, more important, things to think about.

'Harriet,' his voice was caressing, his hands reaching out once more for hers. 'Will you wait for me here in Khartoum, or will you return to England and wait for me there?'

Harriet looked up at him despairingly. 'I shall not be waiting for you at all, Mr Crale.'

Bewilderment flashed across Sebastian Crale's fine-drawn features.

With her hand still held in his she said awkwardly, 'I am very aware of the honour you have done me in asking for my hand in marriage, but I have no desire to marry.'

Sebastian smiled reassuringly. 'I am well aware of the difference in our stations in life. I have taken it all into account and am uncaring of it.'

Harriet gave a small smile. 'That is very gracious of you, Mr Crale.'

'The sooner we break the news the better. There will be storms and tears, but only for a little while. My mother has been urging me to marry for years. This marriage will not be the one she expects but she will grow accustomed to it.'

'You have misunderstood me,' Harriet said, raising her unhappy face to his. 'I was not declining your offer because you are the son of a lord and I am the daughter of a missionary. I was declining it because I truly have no desire to marry.'

Sebastian Crale's face was incredulous. 'But Harriet, I love you.'

Her smile was wan. 'Mr Crale, you barely know me.'

'I know enough to want you for my wife.'

'I am sorry.' Very firmly she disengaged her hands from his and walked swiftly into the shadow of the consulate.

Sebastian stared after her disbelievingly. Instead of being overcome with joy and gratitude, she had turned him down! Him! Sebastian Crale! A man regarded in the highest social circles as an enviable catch in the marriage stakes. A new feeling was born in him. He had asked her to marry him because the idea amused him. Her refusal stirred a stronger, deeper feeling. Miss Harriet Latimer was a rarity and one he would be a fool to let go. There were three days before he sailed south. In three days surely a man of his sophistication would win her heart? He had been too premature in his declaration. He had given her no warning of it: had not paid court to her. With fresh optimism he strode towards his rooms.

For the next three days Harriet found herself besieged. Flowers filled her room; love letters were brought hourly on silver salvers by Jali. A diamond, the like of which Harriet had never seen before, was given as a gift and duly returned. The only safety from his attentions lay in remaining in her room. From her balcony she could see the river bank and, after the expedition to the dockside, could place with ease the three substantial boats being prepared for the trek south. On being asked by Jali if there was anything she required, she asked impulsively for binoculars. They arrived promptly, engraved with her initials – a present from Sebastian that this time she did not immediately return. Despising herself for her weakness, she stood for long hours, watching as boxes and drums of foodstuffs were loaded; as Dr Walther hurried aboard with the sextants and barometers she had seen in his room; as Raoul Beauvais carried aboard books and tightly rolled scrolls that were presumably maps. So her father would have prepared for his expedition if he had been alive. And she would have been with him. Sick at heart she continued to watch until darkness fell.

As the day approached that they were to leave, Sebastian sent frantic notes by Jali and then, to his mother's anguish, knocked personally on Harriet's door, begging her to see him, if only for a moment. Harriet refused.

In the late hours of the final evening inspiration gripped Sebastian. It was because she was not allowed to join the expedition with him that she was behaving so obdurately. He approached Raoul and to the alarm of the other members of the expedition, blows were nearly struck before they had even left Khartoum. Furious and despairing, Sebastian returned to the consulate and the door of Harriet's room.

'I have done everything in my power to insist that you accompany us,' he said helplessly. 'Beauvais is adamant. He says no woman is strong enough for such an expedition and I fear he is right. It would be taking you into danger and I would rather die than do that.'

Harriet remained silent, gazing out towards the dusk-dark river and the creamy sails of the boats.

Sebastian groaned. He had a choice: he was not compelled to travel south. He could stay in Khartoum and continue his wooing of Harriet. He could even return with her to England. Indecision tore at him. Even if he stayed he had no guarantee that Harriet would consent to be his wife. Her stubbornness on the subject had been beyond all understanding. And if he didn't journey with Beauvais he would lose his only chance of glory. Beauvais was the finest leader and most intrepid explorer ever to make the attempt at finding the Nile's source. If any man could succeed Raoul Beauvais could. And he, Sebastian Crale, would stand beside him when he did so. His name would be written in the history books of the world.

He said defeatedly through the closed door, 'Goodbye, Harriet. I shall contact you in England when I return.'

Harriet sensed that the siege to her heart had finally been

abandoned. She opened the door and said softly, 'Goodbye Sebastian. I pray that you will return safely.'

He clasped her hand for a brief moment, his eyes eloquent, and then strode away. Sadly Harriet closed the door and then returned to the now dark balcony. Magdalene loved Sebastian: Sebastian loved her: she loved Raoul Beauvais and Raoul Beauvais loved his little Circassian. Tomorrow he would sail out of her life for ever and she would never see any of them again. Sebastian Crale would not return to England for her. It had been her refusal of his impulsive proposal that had made his courtship over the past days so determined. He did not truly love her. He would forget her the instant Khartoum faded into the distance.

She slept restlessly. If only Raoul had given permission for her to accompany them. She could have suffered his presence in the exhilaration of such a trip. She could have fulfilled her father's dream. His death would not have been entirely in vain.

Rage and misery fought for mastery. How *dare* he refuse her on the grounds that she was a woman and not strong enough? Surely she had proved her stamina travelling without provisions and with a dying man through the heat of the desert? She doubted if Dr Walther had her constitution: or Sebastian Crale. Sleep came only in brief snatches. At the first light of day she was again on the balcony, binoculars raised to her eyes, watching intently as Raoul's magnificent stallion was led aboard. As mules and camels followed, Sebastian arrived with a coterie of servants. A slim, bespectacled man waved greetings and joined him on the deck of the ship. Then, to Harriet's surprise, she saw a young clerical gentleman arrive. She stared; presumably the other man was a scientist or botanist. What contribution could an Anglican priest make on such an expedition?

Her heart leapt as Raoul emerged on deck, greeting the new arrival warmly. Even at such a distance she could feel the magnetism of his attraction. He stood head and shoulders above Sebastian Crale, a darkly handsome man reducing all those around him to insignificance. Native boys scurried about the decks as the boat prepared to sail. A strong wind blew, filling the sails as the boat eased away from the river bank and out into the centre of the broad river. The two barges carrying supplies followed more clumsily. They were setting off on a great adventure and she, Harriet, was left behind for no other reason than that she was a woman.

The white-collared priest and Sebastian stood in the stern, waving to a small group of onlookers who had come to bid them goodbye. The bespectacled gentleman had disappeared below decks. Raoul stood alone in the prow, legs apart, his hands clasped behind his back. He was going. Within minutes he would be lost to view. Something very like panic rose up inside her and then she gasped.

Gracefully a slim figure emerged from below decks. The wind caught her hair, streaming it behind her as she ran lightly across to where Raoul stood, entwining her arm through his. Harriet's heart began to slam in slow, heavy strokes. He had refused her permission to join them on the grounds that she was a woman. He had forbidden her the opportunity of fulfilling not only her own but her father's ambition. Yet a woman *was* to be a member of the party. His statement to Sebastian that the trek was too dangerous for her had been nothing but a ruse to prevent her joining them. He had not wanted the embarrassment of her presence. Narinda would stand at the fountains of the Nile. Narinda who probably had no more interest in the river's source than Lady Crale. She was filled with a rage that was white hot. This time Mr Raoul Beauvais had overreached himself. She snatched clean underclothes and a change of blouse and skirt and rolled them furiously into a pack. She had no need of anything else. Provisions to sustain an army had been taken on board. She grabbed the gun Raoul had given her, and which had lain, discarded, beneath her bed, and then, raced down to the courtyard and across to the stables. The horse was not hers to take but Harriet was beyond caring. It would be returned – eventually.

She galloped hard through the dusty, mud-beaten streets and out into open country. The Nile ran broadly on her right hand side, the sailing boat and barges clearly visible. The ground near the banks was marshy and she had to veer away, riding through groves of acacias, their white bulbous thorns the only relief against the barrenness of the surrounding desert. The strong wind speeded the boats so that she was soon left far behind. They would anchor at dusk: she would catch them up or die in the attempt.

It seemed to her in the following hours that death was going to be her only reward for her foolhardiness. The heat was stunning. She had not even had the forethought to bring water with her and it was obvious that her horse could not continue to gallop indefinitely. Soon she was forced to reduce the animal to a canter and then, as perspiration streamed down both animal and rider, to a walk. Far ahead she could see the shining white of the sails. A stubborn obstinacy drove her on. They would anchor through the night and if she had to walk on her bare feet she would join up with them.

The day was the longest of her life. It stretched out interminably: heat and flies, dirt and exhaustion. When the desert night fell she was filled with fresh fears: fears of the animals that haunted the river banks. Occasionally she heard the slither of crocodiles and sounds of other beasts she could not identify. She touched the stock of her gun for reassurance. If the boats did not anchor through the night then she was lost. Without water her horse would not have the strength to return to Khartoum. She would die alone in the desert as she had so nearly done before.

When the white gleam pierced the darkness she almost sobbed with relief. Urging her horse to further effort she cantered towards the lamp-lit boat. At the sound of her approach confusion broke out. Within seconds a rifle shot missed her by inches and her horse shied in fear. Her cry brought even more shouts from the anchored vessels.

'It's a rider, not an animal!' she heard Dr Walther shouting.

'It's a woman!' Raoul's voice shouted savagely and then she saw his familiar figure vault over the side of the boat and splash through the water and reeds. Semi-conscious with relief she slipped from the back of her lathered horse and was immediately seized by the shoulders so hard that she cried out in pain.

'You little fool! You could have died out there!'

'I nearly did,' she said with an exhausted sob.

'It would have served you damned right!' His eyes blazed into hers. 'If you're trying to wreck my expedition, you've failed miserably.'

'Wreck it?' Harriet gazed up at his furious face dazedly.

'Crale is continuing south and not returning to Khartoum with you!'

'But . . .' Her words were silenced as his fingers dug brutally into her shoulders.

'We are not going to be delayed or lose a member of our party by having you escorted back to safety. You have achieved more than you bargained for, Miss Latimer! You chose to join us. Now you will stay with us.'

Harriet wanted to laugh aloud. She had gained her objective and as far as she cared Raoul Beauvais could labour under whatever delusions he desired.

He shook her viciously. 'You will also discontinue your liaison with Crale until the expedition is over. There is no place for lovemaking on a scientific expedition.'

'Does that apply to the expeditionary leader as well?' she spat viciously, struggling to free herself from his brutal gasp.

'As far as you are concerned, Miss Latimer, utterly.' He let go of her so suddenly that she almost fell.

'My goodness! What on earth . . .?' A bewildered Dr Walther had struggled through the reeds and up the bank to join them.

'Miss Latimer will be accompanying us after all,' Raoul said tersely, turning on his heel and striding into the water to the boat without making the least effort to assist her.

'My dear Miss Latimer . . .' The little doctor's comforting arm was around her. In the darkness Harriet could hear Sebastian Crale's voice raised, first in disbelief and then anger as Raoul informed him of her arrival and then forbade the continuance of any liaison between them. Dr Walther helped her through the reeds and knee-high water and Raoul's voice was heard saying tightly,

'You will do as I say, Crale. You will not delay the expedition by returning Miss Latimer to Khartoum.'

The concerned face of the priest leant over the rails as he stretched out helping hands. Gratefully she took hold of them and then her feet touched the planks of the deck and Sebastian was at her side. She was too tired to face a further explanation as to her conduct. Sebastian would doubtless misconstrue her motives, just as Raoul had.

'I'm tired and thirsty, Sebastian. I have no wish to talk to anyone this evening.'

Dimly she was aware of everyone's concern. Dr Walther's arm never left her shoulders as he ushered her below decks and into a cabin that was obviously his own. The young Anglican priest squeezed in beside him with lime juice and biscuits. The bespectacled man she had not yet been introduced to brought her a fever powder. Sebastian hovered in the doorway, voluble in his anxiety. Only Raoul was absent. As the gentlemen excused themselves, Harriet was aware of another pair of eyes watching her. This time there was no friendliness or concern in them: only open hostility.

Narinda turned swiftly, her ankle-length robes shimmering in the lamplight. Then the cabin door closed and Harriet was alone. She lay on the bunk and closed her eyes. She had achieved her objective: why then did she feel no elation? She was embarking on a voyage that no European woman had ever attempted before. Only weeks ago the prospect would have filled her heart with joy. Now it seemed as if she was capable of feeling only pain. She doubted that Narinda would be sleeping alone in a narrow bunk. Even now she would once again be with Raoul, enjoying his companionship, his rare smiles, his caresses. She clenched her hands into tight little fists. She had known what the situation would be and she had judged it preferable to a return to England. Raoul Beauvais and his Circassian would have to be endured.

It was not an easy task. Narinda made no secret of her close relationship with Raoul, spending long hours kneeling at his feet on the deck of the boat, as they sailed further and further southwards.

Sebastian had been convinced that she had hurried after them because she had undergone a change of heart and wanted to marry him after all. Her insistence that this was not so left him perplexed and almost as bad-tempered as Raoul.

Dr Walther remained permanently affable, bubbling with

enthusiasm for their adventure, bringing Harriet a massive collection of plants and grasses to sketch. Reverend Lane asked to be called by his Christian name of Mark and seemed to combine a healthy dose of common sense among his dreams of exploration. The bespectacled young man was a Mr Wilfred Frome from Chichester, who had been sponsored on the expedition by the Royal Geographical Society of London.

The sailing boat, though considerably larger than the dhow on which they had journeyed to Khartoum, was a small area for seven people to live in, especially when so many were barely on speaking terms with one another. Narinda never deigned even to wish Harriet good day. Raoul and Sebastian spoke to each other only when necessary and their animosity made the other three male members of the party uncomfortable, especially as they had no idea as to its cause. The chill between Raoul and Harriet was obvious to all. It distressed the doctor, puzzled the reverend and bewildered Mr Frome. Sebastian was grateful for it. The Frenchman's reputation with women was notorious. It seemed to him that Harriet showed good sense in avoiding his company.

Day after day the mile-wide expanse of river rolled southwards through dry, hard scrubland with nothing to break the monotony but the whirring of countless insects and the slapping of the waves on the reeds.

At the end of the second week Dr Walther began to flag, complaining of sickness and headaches. Excusing himself, he went below to the small cabin he shared with Wilfred Frome and did not reappear when they anchored and sat down to their evening meal.

The little doctor was not of a complaining nature. Harriet felt the first sharp twinges of apprehension. As soon as the meal was finished she hurried to his cabin and knocked. A barely-recognisable voice forbade her to enter, asking her to summon Raoul. Harriet ignored the request and flung open the door. Dr Walther's kindly eyes were wild. He was shaking violently, the heat coming off his wet skin in waves.

Taking one look at him, Harriet turned and ran for Raoul. He was still at the table, leaning back in his cane chair as Narinda poured him coffee. Harriet ran up to him, grasping his arm in her anxiety. The Circassian girl's eyes flashed. Raoul stared at her in startled amazement. It was the first time she had so much as looked in his direction since he had taken her on board.

'Dr Walther,' she gasped, her face pale. 'I think he has malaria.'

'There's nothing we can do,' he said tersely to Harriet after he had examined the doctor. 'He'll either live or he'll die.'

Harriet stared up at the grim, forbidding face. 'I think,' she said slowly, 'that you are the coldest, most insensitive man I have ever met.'

A brief smile twisted his mouth. 'You may think what you please, Miss Latimer. I don't give a blessed damn.'

He turned once more to the bunk and the convulsively shaking man.

'What are you going to do?'

He turned, looking at her in surprise. 'Nurse him,' he said simply.

Harriet felt a faint flush rise in her cheeks. She had assumed he had cared little for the doctor's health except in regard to how it affected his expedition. She had been wrong. She said awkwardly,

'There is no need. I can do all that is necessary.'

Dr Walther's presence seemed already to have left them. The cabin was so small that her skirt brushed against his legs. Their eyes held and Harriet felt the flush in her cheeks deepen.

'When are you going to marry Crale?' he asked, not taking his disturbing gaze from her.

'I am not,' she said with all the dignity she could muster.

His brows flew together. He tilted her chin with his finger, staring at her challengingly.

'Why? Did his mama disapprove?'

'No doubt she would have done if I had accepted the proposal,' Harriet said stiffly, her heart beginning to race.

His frown deepened. She was so near his body that the scent of her sent his blood coursing through his veins.

'You refused him? Why?'

If she moved the barest inch, her body would be pressed close against his. She strove to retain the cool indifference she had displayed for so long.

'I have no wish to marry,' she said through parched lips.

'Of course not.' His smile was mocking. 'You don't like to be touched, Miss Latimer, do you? I had forgotten how vehemently you requested that I should not do so when you had Lady Crale for a witness.' His eyes moved to her lips. 'Lady Crale is no longer with us, Miss Latimer.' And before she could cry out in protest, he caught her to him, kissing her fiercely and expertly, unaware of the slim, robed figure that slipped away into the shadows.

Vainly Harriet struggled, but he did not release her until he chose to do so. When he did, his eyes were cold. 'Once I believed such kisses came from your heart, Miss Latimer. I was deceived, for you do not possess one. Sebastian Crale is fortunate in his disappointment.'

'You are insolent,' she hissed and slapped his face with all the strength she could muster. He laughed mirthlessly.

'And you are self-seeking. Your only desire is the glory of discovering the Nile's source. For that end you used both me and Crale. You will use me no longer, Miss Latimer.'

She cried out in protest, but he seized hold of her shoulders and propelled her through the cabin door. 'Send Narinda to me,' he ordered curtly. 'I need water and laudanum.'

Harriet found that she was shaking as much as the stricken doctor. How dare he accuse her of being self-seeking? She was doing nothing more than anyone else taking part in the expedition. He was arrogant, cruel and grossly unfair. Her lips felt burned and bruised by his kisses. She had spent the past weeks convincing herself that she had been suffering from a schoolgirl infatuation that was now under control. In one crushing embrace he had destroyed that illusion for ever. Her feelings for him were too intense ever to be under her control.

'Mr Beauvais wishes water and laudanum taken to Dr Walther's cabin,' she said, approaching Narinda where she sat sewing one of Raoul's exquisitely lace-edged shirts.

Narinda raised her eyes from her work and looked at Harriet with such venom that Harriet instinctively stepped backwards.

'You shall not have him,' she said, rising to her feet in a fluid feline movement. 'You shall never have him!' and she moved swiftly away to carry out Raoul's bidding, leaving Harriet shocked and shaken and ashamed of the intensity of her feelings.

'From now on we anchor in midstream of an evening,' Raoul said when he finally emerged from Dr Walther's cabin. 'Perhaps in the centre of the river the mosquitoes will not be so dense.'

'How is Dr Walther?' Sebastian asked, his grey eyes betraying an almost frightened anxiety.

'Sick,' Raoul replied tersely.

Narinda glided to his side, whispering to him in Arabic, her hand resting lightly on his arm, her eyes triumphant as they met Harriet's.

Harriet turned her head away. How did the girl know of her feelings for Raoul? In what way had she betrayed herself?

She said, 'I will nurse Dr Walther through the night,' and without waiting for permission, walked swiftly away, her skirt whipping around her ankles.

The little Circassian had soon left the sick man when Raoul was no longer there. Her behaviour when Raoul was present was markedly different from her behaviour when he was absent. Her berating of the native boys when Raoul was not in earshot amused both Sebastian and Mr Frome. It saddened Mark Lane who thought she should show more Christian charity and angered Harriet. The girl was a shrew with no regard for the feelings of others. How could Raoul be so deceived by her? Her soft words were capable of turning within seconds to tart reprimands. Harriet sponged Dr Walther's fevered brow. Presumably Raoul knew nothing of that side of Narinda's nature, and if he did know, was uncaring.

Daily Dr Walther's condition worsened and daily the air became more humid, the banks greener, the flies more prolific.

'I am dying,' Dr Walther said to her in a moment of lucidity. 'Dying!'

'Nonsense.' Even to her own ears her optimism was hollow.

She tensed as the cabin door opened and Raoul entered. Her nightly nursing of the doctor had gradually became a daytime vigil as well. The natives sailing the *dahabiah* and the barges had become increasingly mutinous and Raoul's attention was devoted to keeping control of the straggle of boats as their way became hampered by rotting vegetation and the river no longer ran smoothly but merged between islands of floating debris and swamps. She had not slept properly for a week. Damp wisps of hair clung to her forehead, curling forward on her cheeks. Her garments were creased and crumpled, her face drawn and exhausted.

He said roughly, 'How long is it since you slept?'

'I don't know. Two days . . . Three . . .'

'I thought Narinda was helping you?'

Harriet's exhausted eyes were astonished. The Circassian had never entered the cabin since Raoul had left it. Raoul's mouth tightened.

'I ordered her to take over from you at eight-hour stretches. Has she not been doing so?'

She most certainly had not, but Harriet was not going to descend to Narinda's level of pettiness. She said tiredly, 'I prefer to nurse the doctor myself.'

'You are on the point of collapse.' His voice held a depth of feeling that startled her. 'Go to your cabin and rest. I will tend the doctor.'

'But Narinda . . .'

'Narinda is no fit companion for a dying man,' he said abruptly.

Harriet's shocked eyes flew to Dr Walther. He was unconscious, shaking convulsively, his clothing and bedding wet with sweat.

'I've tended him as diligently as I did my own father,' she said, a break in her voice.

His hand rested on her shoulder, the hard lines of his mouth softening.

'You have been magnificent,' he said. 'Now rest.'

She gazed up at him wonderingly. His eyes were warm and appraising and she could feel herself succumbing once more to his strange charm. The hand on her shoulder was restraining. She remembered their last encounter in the same cabin. The hurtful words – the brutal kiss.

'Harriet,' he said, and his voice thickened as he drew her towards him.

'Excuse me.' She twisted from his grasp, running from the cabin to her own, locking the door behind her and leaning against it, her heart pounding. Dear Lord, but she had nearly entered his arms of her own volition. Not even the presence of his mistress was enough to save her from temptation. In future she would ensure that she was never alone with him. She would cultivate Mark Lane's company. She would not be so indifferent to Sebastian. His attentions had, at least, been honourable. Her tortured mind sank into the oblivion of sleep.

When she awoke it was evening. She changed one lot of bedraggled clothing for another and brushed her hair vigorously, knotting it into a sleek coil in the nape of her neck. The rest had done her good. Her face no longer looked so pinched or white.

On deck she found Sebastian and Wilfred Frome smoking cigars and dispiritedly discussing the increasing vegetation and swampland into which they were entering.

'Is Mr Beauvais still with Dr Walther?' she asked Mark Lane, who was sitting at a makeshift table calculating the distance they had travelled that day.

'Yes.' He put his pen down. 'I am afraid there is very little hope for his life.'

The air was alive with the sound of insects and fireflies swarmed thickly around the lamp illuminating his work.

Narinda crossed the deck with easy grace, her flowing robes shimmering, a jug of lime juice in her hands as she disappeared below the deck.

'Refreshments for Mr Beauvais,' Mark Lane said with a smile. 'It is truly uplifting to witness such devotion.'

Harriet bit back the sharp retort that rose to her lips. For a man of the cloth Reverend Lane had some peculiar ideas as to what was uplifting.

'Goose for our dinner tonight,' he said. 'Sebastian shot a whole flock of them this afternoon. Ducks as well. Hashim will do us proud.'

'Yes.' She had barely spoken to Hashim since boarding the *dahabiah*. He travelled on the largest of the barges, in charge of stores, cooking and the Sudanese native boys who crewed the vessel. Every evening when they had anchored, the fruits of his labours were transported from the barge to the *dahabiah*. He had expressed no surprise at finding her amongst their party. His sharp black eyes had flicked away from Harriet to Raoul to Narinda and he had returned to his barge grateful that he would be some distance away when the inevitable storm broke.

Harriet moved away and allowed Reverend Lane to continue his calculations. She had no desire to join Sebastian or Wilfred Frome. Mr Frome was already declaring that there could be no navigable channel through the swampland they were entering and Harriet found his pessimism depressing. She walked to the *dahabiah's* prow and stood, gazing down into the black, swirling water. At the moment, at least, a channel was open to them and they were continuing at a reasonable pace. How long it would last no one knew. From the distance came the roar of a prowling lion. She shivered. Hippos had made their way almost impossible at times but she had watched them with fascination. The crocodiles she had long since become accustomed to; the monkeys she had found amusing and the lizards intriguing. But the nightly roars of the lions filled her with nothing but fear. Eventually they would have to leave the boats and continue their journey by horse and mule. There would be no water for protection against the marauding lions: only their wits and their guns. She was so immersed in her thoughts that she was unaware of Narinda stepping quietly once more on to the deck.

The Circassion's lustrous eyes were malevolent. She knew very well of her master's love for the English girl for he had told her of it and of his intentions the minute he had returned to Khartoum. What had happened then Narinda had no way of knowing. She knew only that she had him once more to herself and had exulted in the fact. Now he was turning against her, furiously angry because she had not assisted the English girl in her nursing of the German. She had seen their savage embrace and she knew that every day he was becoming more distant from her, his brooding thoughts centred entirely on the girl who stood before her in the darkness, gazing down into the deep depths of the river.

Narinda glanced behind her. The priest had disappeared, his table empty. In the distance the two Englishmen were talking, a bottle of brandy at their feet; their glasses full. Narinda moved swiftly.

Harriet felt a violent blow in the centre of her back and fell forward, grasping vainly at the shallow rail. As she did so a demon-like push sent her plunging head-first into the ink black river.

She sank in blind terror, kicking and struggling, fighting for survival. Choking on the filthy water, she surfaced, gasping for breath. The darkened shape of the *dahabiah* was already several yards away as she screamed desperately for help. Then, above her screams, she heard the unmistakable slithering of crocodiles down the bank and into the water. Her screams rose, demented with terror.

On the *dahabiah* shouts rang out and lanterns were rushed to the deck rails.

Water closed over head. Monstrous, trailing things caught at her legs, her arms. She fought upwards, breaking the surface once more, screaming his name.

He dived from the prow and as he did so Sebastian and Wilfred Frome shot rifle shot after rifle shot above her struggling head towards the bank at the unseen but approaching predators.

'For the love of God!'

He had her in his grasp and then they both submerged as she clung to him frantically. She felt a sharp blow to her jaw and then nothing until she was hauled like a beached fish aboard the *dahabiah* and laid on the deck, retching and sobbing with fear and relief.

The last rifle shot rang out. Raoul stood above her, panting, water streaming from his hair, his sodden shirt almost transparent.

'Have you no brains?' he yelled, his face contorted with fury. 'I warned everyone of the dangers of falling overboard! You nearly killed us both!'

She pushed her streaming hair from her eyes and struggled into a sitting position.

'I didn't fall in!' she yelled back at him as Sebastian, Wilfred and Mark Lane surrounded them with lanterns held high. 'I was pushed!'

He laughed harshly. 'Who by? The Archangel Gabriel?'

'I don't know by whom, but I can guess!' Her wet skirts clung to her as she rose to her feet.

'Was it Reverend Lane?' he asked with scathing sarcasm. 'Or was it Mr Frome or Sebastian Crale? Or perhaps it was me? Perhaps I threw you overboard for the sheer pleasure of it and then risked life and limb to retrieve you!'

Harriet swivelled round, searching the dark deck. Narinda stood some distance away, her hands folded demurely before her, her long-lashed eyes expressionless.

'By her!' Harriet cried, storming through the circle of men and standing pantingly before Narinda. 'You pushed me!'

Narinda raised delicate eyebrows, stretching her hand out, palm upwards in incredulity. 'I? I have been nursing the good doctor. Why do you speak to me like this?'

'Because you tried to kill me!' Harriet replied, beside herself with fury.

Narinda smiled, disappointed at the failure of her actions but relishing the sight of the English girl's dishevelment. The gloating, mocking smile was more than Harriet could bear. She raised her hand and slapped Narinda soundly across her cheek.

Her arm was wrenched so violently that she nearly fainted as she was whirled around.

'Don't ever lay hands on her again!' In the blood-red light of the lamp he looked like a demon out of hell. 'She has had enough such treatment from the likes of you!' He hurled her away from him and circled the crying Narinda with his arms. Harriet felt as if she were going mad. *She* was the one who had nearly been murdered and the would-be murderess was the one being comforted!

'Have some brandy,' Sebastian was saying, pressing a glass into her hand. She drank the unfamiliar liquid gratefully and then, when Mr Frome refilled the empty glass, she allowed Sebastian to draw her comfortingly close. He, at least, was constant. She said at last,

'I must change.'

He nodded, looking down at her, concern in his eyes. She forced a smile.

'I am quite recovered, Sebastian. There is no need to look so anxious.'

'I was worrying for your safety. I wish to God we had never embarked on this expedition. Walther is dying. We are surrounded by swamps and now you have fallen overboard and nearly drowned.'

She pressed her hands against his chest and pushed herself away. 'I did not fall. That girl pushed me.'

Sebastian smiled affectionately. 'Narinda is as light as a bird. She could not possibly have done so.'

'That bird has claws!' Harriet said tartly and marched indignantly in her soaking skirts to her cabin.

Not even Sebastian believed her. The brief empathy that had grown up between her and Raoul earlier in the day had been extinguished as if it had never existed. Which, she thought as she took off her wet garments, it might very well not have done. She was sure of nothing any longer; except of one thing. She had *not* fallen. She had been pushed and Narinda was the person responsible.

The next day the scenery was nightmarish, the river almost stagnant. Dead trees reared starkly from the water. Vulture-like birds sat menacingly on the branches. There was no clear channel. The river diverged into scores of narrow waterways through head-high papyrus reeds, and rotting vegetation.

'Sudd,' Sebastian said, his face ashen as he eyed the hideous green swamp that surrounded them, stretching limitlessly to the horizon. 'How the devil do we free ourselves of it?'

'By persistence,' Raoul said and Harriet noticed signs of strain on his hard-boned face, for the first time.

She moved past him and he said unexpectedly, 'Where are you going?'

'To Dr Walther.'

He nodded. For once there seemed no anger in him; only intense concentration. If they were to free themselves from the swamp every decision taken had to be the right one and he, and he alone, was the decision maker.

By the evening of the next day Harriet knew that Dr Walther was on the point of death. Weakly she raised herself from his bunkside and went in search of Raoul.

'Is he conscious?' Raoul asked, pushing his compass and papers aside and rising to his feet.

'Barely.' Together they hurried below decks to the cramped, steamy cabin. Dr Walther's eyes flickered open. Weakly he patted Harriet's hand as she knelt beside him.

'She is a good girl,' he murmured. 'A good girl.' There was a faint smile on his lips as Raoul bent over him.

'Goodbye, dear friend,' he said, and his last breath rasped in his throat and ceased.

Harriet covered her face with her hands and began to cry. Lightly, so lightly that afterwards she wondered if it had been her imagination, Raoul touched her hair and turned on his heel.

They buried Dr Walther on the only dry ground that could be found: a tiny island covered with tree lilies, their bouquet of leaves like glistening bayonets. As Mark Lane read the funeral service Sebastian slipped his arm comfortingly around her shoulders and she did not draw away. Since the angry scene between herself and Raoul she had become grateful for his companionship. It was easier to sit and talk with Sebastian in the evenings than to sit alone with nothing to divert her attention from the sight of Raoul and Narinda.

She turned her head away from the sight of Narinda sitting serenely at Raoul's feet as he worked at his papers, and concentrated once more on the game of chess she was playing with Sebastian. She leaned over to move a knight and her bent head came in close contact with Sebastian's. Raoul watched through narrowed eyes and there was a flexing of muscles along his jaw line. She had spurned his advances and encouraged the Englishman. Why then had she not accepted Sebastian Crale's proposal of marriage? It was obvious that he was besotted with her. He saw Sebastian's hand over Harriet's as he guided her next move and he felt the pulse in his temple begin to throb.

Narinda looked up at his grim profile and across to where his eyes rested. The English girl. His thoughts were constantly on the English girl. Tiny teeth bit deeply into her lower lip. She had heard of slavers who had ventured through the swamp in search of victims. Soon they would be in the country of chiefs accustomed to selling their people as slaves: and buying them. The English girl's rarity would ensure that any chief would pay a great price for her. Her eyes gleamed in the darkness. She had acted once on impulse and had failed. The next time she would act with forethought and cunning and would succeed.

Chapter Eight

The unpleasantness of the voyage increased; the climate almost insupportable. The large maps that were constantly spread on the cane table were inked in with strange names. The whole vast area was ringed with the same Sudd and the rivers diverging from it bore enchanting names that gave little indication of their hideousness. Bahr-el-Zeraf, the river of the giraffes: Bahr-el-Ghazal, the river of the antelope. Raoul worked with grim determination, charting their course meticulously, charting their latitude point nightly with the aid of his sextant. Often the natives were reduced to scything the vast banks of reed to enable the *dahabiah* to cut its way inexorably forward. To Sebastian's distaste, Raoul stripped to the waist, and with Reverend Lane helping manfully, joined his natives in hacking a waterway through the dense mass of vegetation.

The sweat poured down his broad back, the muscles rippling as he wielded an axe with demonic ferocity. Sebastian and Wilfred Frome watched from cane chairs, their enthusiasm for the adventure a thing of the past. Harriet watched despairingly. There was nothing she could do to help him. When he staggered back on to the *dahabiah* it was Narinda who ran hastily towards him with towels to wipe the sweat from his face and body. It was almost, Harriet thought as she watched Narinda sponge his forehead with a damp cloth, as if they were man and wife. A humourless smile curved her lips. Almost the first thing Raoul Beauvais had said to her had been that he was not a marrying man. No doubt his present arrangement suited him admirably.

'Is there any possibility of persuading Beauvais to turn back?' Harriet heard Wilfred Frome ask Sebastian.

Sebastian laughed tersely. 'None. He and Walther planned this expedition long ago. He'll continue until he's killed us all.'

Harriet looked ahead to where Raoul worked, waist deep in mosquito-ridden water. He would not kill them. He would succeed – whatever the cost.

Since the undignified incident when she had slapped Narinda's face the girl had made no secret of her hostility towards Harriet but had been careful to cultivate the good humour of the men. Now she moved towards them gracefully, gossamer-light robes fluttering around her as she brought a tray of refreshments for them. Frome blushed slightly, patently overcome by Narinda's obvious charms. Even Sebastian regarded her with appraising eyes. Slowly but surely she was estranging Harriet from everyone aboard. Harriet knew that no one believed Narinda had pushed her overboard. Her slapping of the girl's face had only made matters worse. Raoul saw it as the typical behaviour of a girl of her class to a native, and despised her accordingly. Sebastian and Wilfred Frome's protective instincts had been aroused by the girl's tears. Only Mark Lane remained neutral. Harriet Latimer was not a girl to make wild accusations with no foundation. Neither was she so foolish as to fall over a two-foot rail into water swarming with crocodiles. Though Harriet was unaware of it he kept a close eye on her. Accidents that had happened once could happen again.

Just when it seemed that survival was impossible, Raoul struggled back aboard the *dahabiah* with the natives and said exhaustedly, 'There is a channel ahead. I've been correct in my judgment. We've reached navigable water once more.'

'Thank the Lord,' Mark Lane said sincerely, reaching for his Bible.

'Thank God,' Sebastian said less piously, reaching for a bottle of brandy.

'Thank Raoul,' Harriet said dryly.

He was in the process of washing dried blood from the cuts on his hands. He raised his eyes, giving her a piercing glance that obliged her to turn swiftly before he saw how much it had disconcerted her.

As the river once more became recognisable as such, everyone's spirits lifted, even those of Wilfred Frome. The banks were no longer desolate and deserted. There was wild life in plenty to record and draw: monkeys and beautifully sleek red and white waterbuck, zebras and elephants and once, at early dawn, the breathtaking sight of a cheetah stalking its prey.

There were birds in abundance: spoonbills, stilts, herons, marabou storks, white storks, black storks. So much wild life that they were satiated with it, and Harriet sketched maniacally, reluctant to let even one species escape her pen.

Natives on the banks changed from light-skinned Nubians to ebony-black Africans, their villages clusters of cane and reed-woven huts. Wilfred Frome was eager to put ashore to study the inhabitants as closely as he was studying the flora and fauna. Raoul refused. Their journey back would be the time for Wilfred to collect extraneous data for the Royal Geographical Society. Their chief objective was the Nile's source and they had still not reached Gondokoro, the furthest place ever recorded by white men. Malaria had struck down one of their party: there was no telling when another would succumb. They had plentiful supplies of quinine in which he put much faith. Dr Walther had believed that four bottles of claret a day were ample protection, and had been proved sadly mistaken.

They had sufficient supplies and were able to shoot fresh meat. Delays investigating the native population were unnecessary and potentially dangerous. Every hour of every day mattered. Not until Gondokoro had been reached were they in uncharted territory.

There were times when Harriet wondered when he slept. He captained the *dahabiah*; he kept control over a crew of unhappy and often frightened Sudanese; he mapped the country as meticulously as Wilfred Frome, and his eyes rested on her with increasing and disturbing frequency.

'*Visitors!*' Sebastian suddenly shouted, grabbing his rifle and running to the prow.

Wilfred Frome dropped his pen to the deck as he rose hastily from his notes.

Raoul strode past a startled Harriet, moving with easy strength and confidence. Her sudden fear died; whatever the situation, Raoul would be in control of it. She put down her sketch pad and followed curiously. Canoes full of natives were converging upon them from all sides, their bodies glistening with oil, strips of ochre-coloured cloth about their loins. Only one wore more garments and he stood at the helm of the swiftest canoe, his feet straddled, his spear held upright in one hand. A toga was fastened on one broad, black shoulder and a cape of antelope skins fell around him, ankle length. His face was expressionless, looking to Harriet more like a magnificent wooden carving than a face of human flesh and blood.

'Put your rifle down,' Raoul said authoritatively to Sebastian.

Sebastian hesitated, about to refuse and then, at the expression in Raoul's eyes, unwillingly complied.

The silence had been broken the instant Sebastian had given his warning shout. Drums had begun to pound. Drums that Harriet had heard previously only from a safe distance. Then, they had sounded intriguing and romantic: a sign that they were delving deeper and deeper into the heart of unexplored Africa. Now, near to, the sound was terrifying, full of menace and threat. Every warrior was armed with a lance or a spear and as the drums' rhythm increased, so did their shouts and angry gesticulations.

Raoul faced the chief, standing at the prow of the *dahabiah*, his feet straddled, arms akimbo, as fearless as if he had an army at his back and not a handful of men and two defenceless females.

As the chief's canoe bobbed precariously against the *dahabiah*, Raoul moved forward, speaking in Arabic, his hands outstretched. From the canoe the chief regarded him for long moments while the frenzy around them increased. Harriet pressed her hands against her ears to shut out the sound of drums and cries. Narinda had long since fled, and was cowering in her cabin.

Smoothly Raoul slipped from the obviously uncomprehended Arabic into another tongue. This time there was a faint gleam in the impassive eyes of the chief.

'The beads, Harriet,' Raoul said without turning his head.

Harriet moved quickly. Boxes of brilliantly-coloured necklaces and bracelets had been brought with them for bartering with the local chiefs for food. So far, such bartering had not been necessary. Now she scooped up handfuls of the beaded jewellery and hurried to Raoul's side.

With a sudden flashing smile Raoul dropped them into the chief's grasp. They were caught adroitly. A giant hand was raised and the drums ceased.

Raoul stretched his hand down over the side of the *dahabiah*; the chief looped scores of necklaces over his head and threw the rest to his warriors who caught, seized or dived into the water for them. The black hand and the white clasped and then Raoul was helping the chief aboard and Sebastian's fingers were nervously reaching towards his rifle. Whether Raoul understood what the chief said, and whether the chief understood what Raoul said was unclear. What was clear was that an understanding had been reached and that friendship had been given and received.

'What language is Beauvais speaking?' Sebastian whispered urgently to Wilfred Frome.

Frome shook his head. 'I don't know, but whatever it is, it's doing the trick.' The chief was seated on Raoul's high-backed cane chair and instinctively Harriet hurried for lime juices and glasses. A handful of warriors had boarded with their chieftain and surrounded him, long spears in their hands, while the others remained standing in their rocking canoes.

'What if it hasn't?' Sebastian asked, sweat breaking out on his brow. 'Even with rifles we'd never survive an attack by such a force!'

'Hush . . .' Frome gestured impatiently.

Harriet was approaching with the tray of drinks. Raoul's eyes were reluctantly admiring; she had made the right gesture and it had taken courage to do so. As he sat himself opposite the chieftain it had been Mark Lane who had stepped forward, standing to one side of him.

Raoul curbed a mirthless smile. A priest and a girl had shown more courage than a self-declared hunter. Sebastian Crale was conspicuous only by his absence, as was the other person aboard who had previously been all too eager to meet the natives at close quarters. Raoul dismissed them from his mind. Already he was beginning to feel an almost unquenchable excitement.

The chief before him had declared himself to be Nbatian and regarded the question as to his knowledge of the river's source with indifference. 'In the Nyanzas,' he said. 'It flows from the bowels of the Great Nyanzas.'

Harriet set the drinks down on the table between the two men. The chief's eyes flicked over her, narrowing as they rested on her halo of golden hair.

She heard Raoul use the name Gondokoro and Nyanza, and waited a foot or two from his left-hand side as the chief scored a map on the bottom of the wooden tray with his nails.

Raoul was leaning forward, his shoulders tense, his eyes gleaming. Harriet bit her bottom lip. Was the chief telling him in what direction to travel once their way on the river became impossible, and they could no longer follow its course?

She could sense Raoul's rising excitement and her own began to grow. She had never doubted that he would achieve his objective, but she had begun to doubt if the rest of them had the endurance to share with him the first sight of the Nile's source. Now, suddenly, it seemed not only a possibility, but a certainty.

The chief's fist slammed hard on the table, sending a glass crashing to the floor. Harriet gasped, flooded with fear. He had risen to his feet and was pointing at her, his voice demanding.

Raoul remained seated, shrugging dismissively. The chief's anger grew. Harriet saw the hands of the warriors tighten on their spears.

'What is it? What does he want?' she asked, terrified that Raoul was on the point of death.

With almost insolent ease Raoul swung round in his chair and regarded Harriet calmly as the chief jabbed his finger in her direction.

'He wants you for a wife.'

Harriet's eyes widened, her mouth rounding in horror. 'What . . . What have you told him?' she gasped, backing away in fear.

'I told him,' he said darkly, 'that I was sorely tempted to allow him to have you for one.'

For a second Harriet could not speak because of the pounding of her heart and her stupefying fear. Then anger surged through her.

'Tell your ... your ... *friend*,' she hissed, 'that I am no man's wife!'

Raoul regarded her with infuriating complacency. 'He seems to think that you are mine,' he said, and this time there was no mistaking the mocking gleam in his eyes.

'I'd rather be his than yours!' Harriet spat, her gold-green eyes feral in their fury.

'That can easily be arranged,' Raoul said, leaning back negligently in his chair.

Tears of anger and rage stung her eyes and she choked on them as she said, 'You wouldn't care a damn, would you?'

Black brows rose imperceptibly. 'There's no need for profanities, Miss Latimer.'

Harriet was shaking. She had known fury in plenty since meeting Raoul Beauvais but nothing to equal the almost manic frenzy that now seized her. She was oblivious of the animal-skinned chief, oblivious of the armed warriors, oblivious of Wilfred Frome's pale face and desperate pleas for restraint.

In a blood-red haze she saw only Raoul, lazily mocking her humiliation.

'You are unspeakable!' she sobbed, swirling round, pushing her way between near-naked muscular warrior's as if they were no more than a crowd of children. Raoul regarded her retreating back with interest and returned his attention to his dissatisfied guest.

'I've never known anyone so *arrogant!* So *insolent!* So *unforgivably rude!*' With each adjective she punched her fists into her pillows with such viciousness that feathers scattered around the tiny cabin.

'For God's sake, you nearly got us all killed,' Sebastian said, panting at the cabin door, his face white. 'What did you have to react like that for? I thought that old devil was going to have the lot of us speared. He nearly did for Beauvais after you raged off.'

'I'm very sorry that he didn't!' Harriet yelled, her face smeared by tears, her hair falling unpinned, her breasts heaving.

Desire took a firm hold of Sebastian. Calm, Harriet was undeniably beautiful: enraged, she was magnificent. He moved towards her and as he did so Harriet halted in her tirade, listening tensely. From the distant deck there came a roar of bellowing laughter. It was not Raoul's laugh; or Wilfred's; or Mark's. It could only be the chieftain. The Beauvais charm was working once again.

Sebastian breathed a sigh of relief. 'He's got the old devil eating out of the palm of his hand.'

'Oh, get out!' Harriet shouted exasperatedly, throwing the pillow and its escaping contents at his head. He blinked in surprise, ducked and slammed the door behind him. Lovemaking would have to wait; but not for long. Beauvais had Narinda constantly at his side. He was in no moral position to dictate to other members of the party. Sebastian was filled with fresh resolve. He had been a fool not to continue his assault on Harriet's affections. He would be a fool no longer. Even his mother could not dismiss as unsuitable a girl of Harriet's courage and remarkable spirit.

Raoul, who knew very well where Sebastian had been, regarded him through narrowed eyes, his mouth set in a tight line of pain. Crale was looking uncommonly pleased with himself. No doubt Harriet had thrown herself into his arms in a storm of tears, and been suitably comforted. He had an overwhelming desire to throttle Sebastian Crale. His guest was demanding to be shown the intricate workings of a compass. A pulse ticked angrily at his jaw as he tore his eyes from Crale and obliged.

The meeting with Chief Nbatian livened up Wilfred Frome's spirits considerably. He asked that Harriet sketch every detail of the chief's costume, the canoes, the warriors, the spears. Harriet obliged, keeping as far from Raoul as was humanly possible. On occasions when their eyes did meet she treated him with such withering contempt that it would have shrivelled a lesser man. Raoul merely continued his tasks with indifference.

Sebastian spent long hours sitting beside her as she worked, cleaning his guns, speculating on the credibility of what Nbatian had told Raoul of the great Nyanzas. Harriet sketched furiously and barely heard a word he said. Narinda was growing increasingly annoyed. She spilled vegetable oil on Harriet's skirt, declaring profusely that it was an accident, her eyes belying it. She crept into Harriet's cabin and removed her hair brush, tossing it overboard, denying she knew of its whereabouts when Harriet asked. She found snakes in her bed and, on one occasion, when she left her sketchpad, found the drawings torn from it on her return.

When Harriet accused Narinda of being the perpetrator, Raoul insultingly said that snakes were a hazard they all faced and that no doubt the wind had blown her drawings away. Harriet gritted her teeth and refrained from boxing Narinda's ears with superhuman effort.

Raoul became daily more abrasive and unapproachable and soon it was only Mark Lane who was able to converse with him with any degree of civility.

They stood side by side in early morning light as groves of lemon trees heralded Gondokoro. 'The trek will be trebly difficult once we leave the boats,' Mark Lane said quietly. 'We need to be all of one mind, and journey in friendship, not hostility.'

Raoul remained silent, his brows pulled together, his mouth a hard line.

'It is days since you spoke at any length with Sebastian or Wilfred,' Mark Lane continued, his young face concerned, his Bible in his hands. 'They are becoming restless and disillusioned. I can see no success until the gulf is breached.'

'Neither of them were asked to accompany me,' Raoul said tersely. 'Crale hasn't contributed an ounce of effort to the planning of the expedition or its execution.'

'Then why is he amongst us?' Mark Lane asked with a puzzled frown.

'Because if he had been left behind I would have been refused permission to leave Khartoum.'

Mark Lane remembered that Sebastian's father was the British consul in Khartoum and pursued the subject of Sebastian no further. 'And Frome?'

'The Royal Geographical Society of London requested that he should travel with me. I agreed. I even thought he might prove useful. I had expected a well-seasoned explorer, not an academic.'

'And Miss Latimer?' Mark Lane asked tentatively.

The black brows met satanically. 'Miss Latimer is Sebastian's problem, not mine,' he said and wheeled on his heel, leaving Mark Lane alone as the deserted mission church of Gondokoro came into view.

Harriet shivered as they stepped ashore. There was something eerie about the desolate, crumbling church. Only a giant cross remained intact. What kind of men had forged their way through the swamp of the Sudd to settle here in the hope of converting the heathen? Whoever they had been, they had not survived.

It took three days for the provisions that were to be taken with them to be sorted and packed ready for transport on the camels. The horses were for Raoul, Sebastian and Harriet to ride. The mules had been Wilfred and Reverend Lane's personal choice of transport. Narinda, to her inner fury, had also been allocated a mule and her hatred of Harriet grew. The English girl would ride a horse, as would her master. She, Narinda, would not be accorded such an honour.

As scientific books and instruments were separated from spices and oils, she saw her master's eyes return again and again to the English girl. The English girl pretended not to notice, working feverishly, but Narinda was not deceived. She knew that Harriet was as aware of Raoul's burning glances as she herself was.

Though the church was deserted, Gondokoro was not. There was a handful of slave traders, men so bestial that Harriet felt physically sick at the sight of them. On the day before they were to leave, a convoy of slaves was brought in for shipment to Khartoum. Their chief had sold them willingly and accompanied the heavily-bearded traders as they rode into the collection of miserable dwellings that had arisen around the church.

'If I were a man,' Harriet said passionately to Sebastian, 'I'd shoot those traders myself!'

Sebastian shifted uncomfortably, in no doubt that she would. As in Khartoum she had demanded that he intervene and set the hapless captives free. Sebastian, knowing that any such attempt on his part would result in his death, had refused with as good a grace as possible. Harriet had not been understanding.

'If you will not free them then I will!'

The slaves stood by the river bank, wooden yokes around their necks, their hands and feet cruelly shackled.

'Harriet, please be reasonable.'

Harriet had no intention of being reasonable. To Sebastian's alarm she marched furiously to where the half-drunk and blaspheming traders sat on up-turned water casks, congratulating themselves on their human acquisitions.

Sebastian was not a fool. He knew his limitations. He alone could not rescue her from her headstrong folly. He ran to where the *dahabiah* was berthed, shouting frantically to Raoul as he checked stocks of quinine and morphia. Raoul raised his head, regarding him without interest.

'Harriet is intent on freeing the slaves,' Sebastian yelled from the bank. Raoul's disinterest fled. He slammed down the lid of the medicine chest and vaulted over the side of the *dahabiah*, wading through the water and reeds. As he marched across the wilderness that separated him from Harriet and the traders he checked his pistol. The men Harriet had gone to do battle with were men who regarded rape as a mere diversion and murder as a sport. On their arrival he had silently thanked his Maker that no slaves had been present and on this, their last day, when more traders had entered Gondokoro with their victims, he had ordered that none of his party should have anything to do with them. It was a warning that everyone had heeded. Even Mark Lane had thought only to pray for the souls of those who had perpetrated such crimes and for their abject victims. He should have known, he thought grimly, as he approached the odour of stale sweat and brandy, that Harriet would not be content with mere prayers.

The traders surrounded her, huge bull-necked men with bristly beards and rhino whips at their hips. Harriet's pale gold hair barely reached their chests. Her eyes were blazing, her small body consumed with a fury that freed her from fear.

'There are women and children over there who are being kept shackled, unable to move for hours! They have had no food, no water, no shade! I demand that you free them!'

The roar of laughter was deafening as she stamped her foot, her meaning clear, her eyes brilliant with tears of anger and frustration.

'Have you no Christian conscience? Half of those you intend to sell in Khartoum will never survive the voyage. They are half dead already! Free them. You have ivory in plenty.' She gestured towards the huge pile of tusks that lay a little way from them.

The men were Dutch and their salacious remarks as they ignored her protests, their eyes roving her body, were lost on Harriet. They were not lost on Raoul.

'Return to the boat,' he said tersely to her.

A dozen pairs of blood-red eyes and a pair of flashing gold-green ones swung in his direction.

'I will not! Not until those slaves are freed!'

'No one demands of us,' a guttural voice said in broken English. 'Especially not a woman.'

'Then I *ask* you,' she said vehemently. 'Free the women and children at least!'

'The women bring in as much money as the men,' the Dutchman said lazily. There were warts on his lips and flies crawled unheedingly across his giant bull-head.

Harriet struggled to control her breaking voice. 'I beg you! Free the women and children, *please!*'

'You must forgive my wife,' Raoul said easily, taking out cigars from his shirt pocket and handing them around. 'She is the daughter of a missionary and her ideals make life tedious.'

Harriet gasped. 'How *dare* you . . .'

He seized her wrist, silencing her in mid-sentence. 'Return to the boat,' he said, and at the menace in his voice, the ferocious expression in his eyes, Harriet felt sick.

'I hate you!' she hurled at him. 'You are no better than the traders! And you . . .!' She whirled to face the amused men, '. . . you are scum! Lower than the lowest animal!'

Wrenching her wrist away from Raoul's grasp, she treated him to such a look of contempt that even the hardened traders flinched and then she marched back towards the *dahabiah*, her skirts whipping around her ankles, her head held high.

'My wife,' Raoul said carelessly, sitting down and accepting the brandy bottle that was offered to him, 'is as hot in temper as she is in sex.'

The ensuing laughter succeeded in diffusing the situation. Raoul discussed ivory tusks and his own hopes of procuring a large shipment to take back to Khartoum. The traders complained of the lack of cooperation from local chiefs, apart from the one who stood silently in their midst, regarding Harriet's retreating back with speculative eyes.

'I lost over half my crew in the Sudd,' Raoul lied, wiping his mouth with the back of his hand and passing the bottle to the man beside him. The eyes around him sharpened. 'I'll take some of the slaves off your hands, if you are agreeable.'

'They are fit and strong,' the Dutchman lied. 'They will sell well in Khartoum.'

Raoul regarded the semi-conscious negroes disbelievingly. 'They are dying on their feet.' He leaned forward, his face speculative. 'I'll give you thirty Maria Theresa sovereigns for the lot.'

'What use are the women and children to you?' a voice asked suspiciously.

Raoul shrugged. 'I have a wife. The men in my party do not. Of what use do you think they should be?'

There was more laughter.

'As for the children, it's not worth your while to ship them to Khartoum alone. Your time would be better spent gathering a fresh shipment.'

'A hundred sovereigns.'

'Fifty.'

'Seventy-five.'

'No.' Raoul rose to his feet. 'They're most likely ridden with disease anyway.'

'Sixty,' the wart-faced man said.

Raoul nodded, and shook the outstretched hand. The bargain was sealed. It had cost him a fortune and even as the bewildered negroes were herded on to the provision barges, he was not sure why he had done it. Certainly he had to silence Harriet before the situation grew ugly, but he could have done that and still spared himself the expense of buying every last one of the abject human beings who regarded him from frightened eyes.

'It's unspeakable of him,' Harriet said chokingly to Mark Lane.

Mark Lane laid a restraining hand on her arm. 'Raoul has bought them only to free them.'

She stared up at him.

He smiled. 'Surely you did not think otherwise? What use would three score men, women and children be? When the traders have left Gondokoro the boats will sail the few miles from Gondokoro to the rapids and then they will be set ashore. As for the other calumny that you refer to, he called you his wife in order to afford you protection. As such you would be far less likely to be molested than if you were a single woman with no legal protector.'

Harriet continued to stare. Mark Lane laughed. 'I do not understand you, Harriet. You think only the worst of Mr Beauvais. His intentions are always honourable.'

The lovely line of her jaw tightened. 'On that subject, Reverend Lane, I beg to differ.' She turned away from him, walking rapidly to a grove of lemon trees.

Wilfred and Sebastian had long been in conversation with one another and were now approaching Raoul. Mark Lane bowed his head and said a private prayer for the slaves aboard the barges and for the dead priests who had once inhabited the ruined church.

Occasionally Harriet raised her head from her task and saw that Narinda was standing once more like a shadow at Raoul's side. Her attention was caught as she heard Sebastian's voice rise in anger.

'We none of us realised what the climate would be like before we set off! We shall none of us survive if we travel further!'

'Then return,' Raoul was saying in a bored voice. 'The boats can continue no more. There are cataracts in little over a mile. From now on our journey is overland.'

'Miss Latimer would not survive such hardships!'

'Miss Latimer was not invited.'

Slowly Harriet approached, baskets of lemons in either hand. 'Invited or not, Miss Latimer is continuing,' she said, her face pale, her eyes determined.

Raoul quenched his surge of admiration and said to Sebastian, 'If you wish to return the boats are at your disposal. I ask only that you send fresh vessels through to wait for us here.'

Sebastian struggled inwardly for several moments and then said with bad grace, 'I'll continue,' adding defensively, 'but only for the sake of Miss Latimer.'

Later, when the stores from the vessels had all been landed and the horses and mules exercised, Raoul went in search of Harriet.

She was alone, her head raised, the long, lovely line of her throat clearly defined as she gazed up at the giant cross that hung above the mission church.

'I think,' he said curtly, 'that Crale is right. It would be better for you to return.'

She turned to face him, fighting to keep her voice steady. 'But I have no wish to do so.'

There was a strange note in his voice. 'And I have no wish to have your death on my hands.'

She was about to flash a quick retort but her anger had deserted her, leaving her defenceless. He stood before her, straight and tall, and she was overcome by the desire to reach out and touch him. She said hesitantly, her voice barely audible,

'Would my death matter very greatly, Mr Beauvais?'

His eyes lingered on her lips. He longed to seize her, kissing her until he lost his breath in the sweetness of her mouth. Instead, he said, aware of the harsh edge to his voice,

'It would be an inconvenience, Miss Latimer.'

Harriet clenched her hands at her side, her nails digging painfully into her palms. 'I will do my best not to inconvenience you, Mr Beauvais,' she said stiffly, returning her gaze once again to the cross, blinking back the tears that threatened.

He hesitated. It would be so easy to reach out for her; feel the softness of her body; the sweet smell of her hair. He stepped forward and slowly lowered his hand to her shoulder. Harriet stifled an inarticulate cry. His touch seemed to flame through the lawn of her blouse, burning her body like fire. She felt shameless, her whole being crying out in a need that was primeval. Gently he turned her to face him and she could see the heat at the back of his dark eyes as he studied her face and then he was drawing her into the circle of his arms and she was going as unprotestingly as a dove into the cote.

'Mr Frome is looking for you. His map of the stars has been lost.' Narinda's bell-like voice broke in on them, shattering the private world they had entered.

Momentarily his hands tightened their grasp on her and then released her. His anger at the untimely interruption was too violent to be given expression to. Eyes brilliant with suppressed fury, he swung on his heels and marched through the long grass to where Wilfred floundered amongst a maze of packing cases.

Harriet folded her arms across her breast in an effort to still the trembling that seized her body. One touch, one look of burning desire and all her anger had fled. She had been helpless. As ready to enter his arms as she had been before she had known of Narinda's existence. She pressed her hands to her throbbing temple. Where had all her resolutions gone? Her common sense?

Across the wilderness Narinda stood motionless, her gossamer-light robes falling in soft folds to her feet. Her hands were lowered and clasped in front of her in the manner she often adopted. To the gentlemen of the party, it was a pose that was modest and becoming and, when accompanied by a gentle lowering of her head, a pose that brought protective instincts to the fore. It did not do so in Harriet. So Narinda had stood after trying to drown her. So she stood now – to an onlooker quietly respectful in Harriet's presence. No onlooker saw the gleam of malevolent hate in the lustrous dark eyes as Harriet once more gained control of herself and became aware of Narinda's continuing presence.

The eyes of the two girls met. Harriet's anguished and tormented at her inability to sustain her anger and contempt of Raoul Beauvais; Narinda's feral in their malignancy.

'You shall not have him!' she spat. 'You shall never have him!'

Harriet's heart began to beat fast and light. They were words she had heard before from Narinda. Words spoken before the unsuccessful attempt on her life.

'I have no desire for him,' she lied through parched lips and walked with pounding heart towards the *dahabiah* and the litter of straw.

'You should rest,' Sebastian said assiduously as he checked his rifle. 'You look all in.'

Harriet did not reply. Outwardly composed, her inner emotions were in turmoil. Was this what she had descended to? Squabbling with Narinda over a man faithful to neither of them. When Raoul's powerful figure left Wilfred Frome's side and began to stride in her direction, she swung around so swiftly that the lemons she had been sorting tumbled to the ground. Blindly she hurried in the direction of Mark Lane. Behind her she heard Raoul call her name, and she broke into a run. She could not face him again. Her upbringing, her commonsense, were no protection against the power he exercised over her. Her only salvation lay in avoiding his presence and not allowing her eyes to meet his. Somehow she had to regain her anger. It was her only defence against her true feelings.

Mark Lane slipped a band around the papers he had been rolling and noted her discomposure. Swiftly he looked beyond her and saw the reason for it. Raoul Beauvais stood panting, arms akimbo, his white shirt gashed to the waist, his eyes fixed tormentedly on Harriet's firmly turned back.

He frowned. The hostility between Harriet and Raoul was occasioned by more than her uninvited presence. He wondered, not for the first time, what was its true source.

'Is something disturbing you, Harriet?' he asked quietly, selecting books that could not be left behind.

'Yes . . . no . . .' She hesitated. Mark Lane was a man of the cloth. A man accustomed to hearing and easing emotional burdens. Her cheeks warmed. She could not say that she was in love with a man who openly flaunted his mistress. A man who had taken disrespectful advantage of her. She said stiffly,

'It is the heat. Nothing more.'

Mark Lane's frown deepened. Harriet Latimer was not a very accomplished liar. A dozen yards away Raoul's brows met satanically and then he pivoted on his heel, berating the natives for their inefficiency in unloading the stores.

Amidst much clamour and shouting from the Sudanese, the horses and mules were finally packed with all the provisions and equipment that they were to take with them. Harriet's heart faltered as she listened to Raoul checking aloud from the list he held in his hands.

'Rifles, revolvers, Colts carbine, ammunition for two years, swords, chronometers . . .'

Ammunition to last two years! She felt giddy and faint. Was that how long their expedition would last? Was that how long they would have to live in each other's company, Narinda perpetually between them?

'Prismatic compasses, thermometers, sundial, sextants . . .'

Hashim was returning to Khartoum on one of the barges. She could, if she wanted, return with him.

'Telescope, boxes of mathematical instruments, tents, camp beds, mosquito nets . . .'

Raoul's voice continued as Sebastian chalked crosses on all the appropriate boxes.

'Cooking utensils, camp chairs, blankets, fishing tackle, lanterns . . .'

Her fate lay in her own hands. She could continue into the unknown or she could board the barge.

'Medicine supplies, brandy, tea, soaps . . .'

Her father's dream was within her reach. If she returned his death would have been in vain.

'Spices, oil, sugar . . .'

At last the interminable list came to an end. Earlier she had said that she wished to continue. She was not going to go back on that decision. Hashim bade them goodbye with a face-splitting smile. The porters picked up their bundles and carried them on their heads. Narinda mounted her mule and Sebastian led Harriet to her horse.

'Is your mind quite made up, Harriet? We could return to Khartoum. Marry . . .'

Raoul had wheeled his horse around and was engaged in deep conversation with Narinda. As they parted she saw his strong hand close over the delicately boned one. She fought an onrush of tears and said stiffly,

'My mind is made up, Sebastian,' and then she set her hat on her hair, adjusting the veiling, and rode after Wilfred and Mark Lane.

Raoul was at their head, Narinda at his side. Sebastian at the rear, the porters behind him. As they moved off into land from which no white man had ever returned, the porters began to chant rhythmically. It was a sound Harriet was to associate with Africa for the rest of her life.

Several times Raoul turned in his saddle, his eyes seeking Harriet's, but she always averted her head, staring steadfastly in any direction but his.

In the days that followed the terrain grew more treacherous. The ground was too rocky for the mules to traverse with their heavy baggage and time and time again it had to be manually unloaded and carried, the mules coerced down the sides of steep ravines and up again.

On every hilltop Harriet searched vainly for flat ground and found none. The ravine-filled country was relieved only by sharp spiked bushes and thorns.

It was Sebastian who first saw the village. It was dark and the sun was losing its heat.

'Over there!' he shouted excitedly, galloping past Harriet and on to Raoul. 'A village! Can you see?'

Raoul reined in, his eyes narrowing.

'With a bit of luck they'll be able to tell us more about the Great Nyanzas!' Sebastian said, his fatigue momentarily forgotten.

'And with bad luck they'll prove to be Nyam-Nyams,' Raoul replied drily.

'What are Nyam-Nyams?' Harriet heard Wilfred Frome asking nervously.

Raoul gave one of his rare smiles. 'Cannibals,' he said and urged his horse forward once more.

The village was a collection of conical-shaped cane-woven huts and as they neared it Raoul halted again. 'I think it best if only two of us enter it until we are certain of our welcome.'

'I endorse that decision,' Wilfred Frome said overeagerly.

Raoul's eyes flickered across to him and their expression was contemptuous.

'So do I,' Mark Lane said, cantering to Raoul's side. 'The porters are most uneasy. I think it would be bad policy to enter with them. If they desert our expedition will be at an end.'

Raoul slipped from the saddle. 'Tomorrow will be soon enough for hospitality. I want to have my wits about me when I do enter.'

'Who will be your companion?' Mark Lane asked, wiping a rivulet of sweat away from his clerical collar.

Raoul grinned. 'Frome. He's the Royal Geographical Society's official representative. Detailed descriptions of a cannibal tribe should be just what they are after.'

Wilfred Frome paled and stuttered but Raoul ignored him.

'Let's make camp quickly before we are seen. We don't want unexpected visitors during the night.'

Harriet dismounted and leaned weakly against her horse, closing her eyes. The heat and the flies had been almost unbearable, the rough terrain a constant hazard.

'Are you all right?'

Her eyes flew open. He had not approached her since she had so pointedly turned her back on him at Gondokoro.

'Perfectly,' she snapped and summoning all her strength strode away from him, her skirts swishing around her ankles.

The muscles of his jaw flexed and tightened and then he swore and marched in the direction of the porters, issuing orders tersely.

At first light Raoul and a reluctant Wilfred Frome set off on horseback for the village. Sebastian paced the camp nervously.

'Whatever else the man is, he certainly isn't a coward.'

'Nor kind,' Harriet said, trying to stifle her own anxiety. 'He knew Wilfred had no desire to journey with him.'

'What one risks, we should all be prepared to risk,' Mark Lane said quietly.

Harriet clenched her hands tightly at her side, the nails digging in her palms. What he was risking was his life. She curbed the overriding desire to saddle her horse and ride after him. To do so might only endanger him more. Her lovely face was pale and drawn as she stood tensely, watching the two mounted figures disappear into the distance.

Mark Lane surveyed her with a worried frown and suddenly knew the answer to the question that had been bothering him for so long. It was not hostility that Harriet Latimer felt for Raoul Beauvais. It was love. He smiled to himself. He had seen the expression in Raoul's eyes when they had rested on Harriet and he had thought no one was observing him. The torture in the dark depths was that of a man yearning after what he could not have. When Raoul returned from his expedition, he would speak to him. Whatever the barrier between himself and Harriet, it was not insurmountable. Not when both loved the other with such intensity.

The hot silence was broken by the sudden sound of drums. Sebastian whirled round, snatching up his rifle. Mark Lane restrained him.

'They are not war drums. They are drums of welcome.'

Sebastian relaxed slightly. A tight band circled Harriet's chest so that she could scarcely breathe. What if Mark Lane were wrong? What if even now Raoul was facing death? She moved away from the two men and bowed her head, praying silently.

The drums were still pounding when the two men finally emerged in the shimmering heat of the midday sun, galloping hard back to camp. Harriet sank weakly on to a packing case. He was not dead.

He was alive. He was returning. Even as she watched Narinda ran fleet-footedly to meet him. Desolation swept Harriet's heart. He was returning, but to Narinda, not to her.

Unsteadily she rose to her feet and struggled for composure. Raoul's eyes were exultant. He was out of the saddle before the horse had scarcely halted. 'We're in luck,' he said buoyantly to Mark Lane. 'Chief Latika was both friendly and helpful.' He pulled a canvas chair towards a portable table and spread the map for them all to see. 'One of the great Nyanzas is obviously the Lake Speke discovered last year and named after the Queen. The other, the unknown lake, is known to Latika as the Luta N'zige, Dead Locust Lake, and is in this direction.' His finger moved decisively over the uncharted map.

'But that's over two hundred miles,' Sebastian exclaimed.

Raoul grinned. 'If it were nearer, it would have been discovered long ago.'

'Is that where you believe the Nile springs from?' Mark Lane asked, studying the map with rapt attention.

'I'm almost sure of it.'

'It's almost on the line of the Equator,' Harriet said, bending her head low to see clearly.

Raoul lifted his head and their eyes met. This time Harriet did not turn away. She could not. It was as if, for a split second, they were once again in complete empathy.

'Latika says there are great mountains to the south of the lake.'

'The Mountains of the Moon,' Harriet whispered incredulously.

He nodded and then Sebastian was regaling him with questions and Narinda, seeing the brief exchange between her master and the English girl, slid determinedly between Raoul and Mark Lane, kneeling once more at Raoul's feet.

Harriet's elation died. Incredibly, for an instant of time, she had forgotten Narinda's existence.

'Chief Latika wishes to extend his hospitality to all our party,' Raoul was saying to Mark Lane. 'Tomorrow you and Sebastian will accompany me and Frome will stay in camp with Miss Latimer and Narinda.'

His head was once more bent over the map. His hair had begun to grow low in the nape of his neck. Whereas Sebastian's good looks had wilted with the heat and hazards of the journey, Raoul's had flourished. It was as if he thrived on hardship and danger.

Harriet tore her eyes from the down-bent head of dark springy curls and moved away, busying herself with stitching a skirt that had been rent with thorns. She had no intention of remaining in camp with Wilfred Frome and Narinda. If Sebastian and Mark Lane were to be given the privilege of meeting Chief Latika, then she was going to accompany them.

For the rest of the day Sebastian monopolised her attention, speculating endlessly on the distances involved, the fame such a discovery would bring them, the honours that would follow in its wake.

Raoul, wishing to speak to Harriet alone, curbed his impatience and spoke in private to Mark Lane of other things Latika had told him: of the hostility of the tribes that lay between them and their destination; of the inter-tribal warfare that raged; of the rains that would come and flood the tributaries of the Nile, making their way impassable.

'When will you tell Frome and Crale?' Mark Lane asked, his face sombre.

'When the obstacles become obvious. If I tell them now they will not believe me and think that I am only trying to rob them of the glory they both so much want. Time alone will show if they are worthy to be recorded as the first men to stand at the source of the Nile.'

Mark Lane nodded unhappily. Like Raoul he doubted if Sebastian Crale would be able to withstand prolonged hardship and like Raoul, he had no very great respect for Wilfred Frome's talents as a geographer.

That night Sebastian and Wilfred slept deeply, dreaming of great financial rewards for their endeavours. Raoul slept soundly, encouraged by Chief Latika's verification of the existence of a great lake giving birth to the Nile. Mark Lane prayed and slept with a clear conscience and Harriet slept the sleep of exhaustion. Only Narinda remained awake.

Stealthily she crept into Harriet's tent and snipped off a lock of unbraided golden hair. Then she ran silently across to her mule, leading it some distance from the camp before mounting. Her master had confirmed that the tribe in the village were friendly. She would come to no harm. She knew the English girl better than her master did. She would not stay behind while the others visited Chief Latika. She would accompany them and by so doing would make Narinda's task easier. She smiled to herself in the darkness. Tomorrow would be the last day the English girl disturbed her master's peace of mind. Tomorrow Chief Latika would take the English girl as a slave and she would have her master to herself. She urged her mule onwards, confident that her plan could not fail.

Chapter Nine

At first light the following morning Sebastian and Mark Lane checked their pistols and saddled their horses. Raoul strode to meet them, his body taut, his face grim. Even since the brief moment when his eyes had met Harriet's above the makeshift map he had determined to speak to her alone. Sebastian Crale's presence at her side had made that impossible. He rammed a rifle down his saddlebag bad-temperedly. *Mon Dieu*, but what was the matter with her? She blew hot and cold with the variability of her country's climate. He swung himself up into his saddle. Wouldn't it be better if she remained cold? If he did not speak to her? Surely, in time, his passion would become controllable? Would stultify and die? He had never before desired marriage. He had desired only his freedom. Why should a golden-haired English girl make that freedom meaningless?

She emerged from her tent looking as neat and trim as if she were about to pay an afternoon visit with her aunts. Her hair was brushed to a gleaming sheen and coiled in thick plaits in the nape of her neck. Her blouse was demurely high-necked, the full sleeves fastening tightly at the wrists with small, pearl buttons. Her skirts fell in soft falls from a hand-span waist. Her boots, dust-covered from the endless treks up ravines too steep for her horse to carry her, had been scrupulously polished. An emotion he had never encountered before surged through him, holding him rigid. If he married Harriet Latimer he had no need to forsake Africa or his dreams of exploration. She would accompany him, be at his side, revelling in the adventure of charting an unknown continent.

With perfect composure she set her broad-brimmed hat firmly on her head and, without assistance, mounted her horse.

Raoul's frown deepened. 'Where,' he asked, a dangerous note in his voice betraying some of the feelings he had suffered for the past weeks, 'do you think you are going?'

'With the expedition to the village,' Harriet replied with a confidence she did not feel.

A slight tic appeared at his jaw line. 'You will remain here. An initial overture of friendship indicates very little. Our reception may be very different today.'

'Then I will ride with you and see for myself,' Harriet replied with infuriating politeness.

The temper Raoul had kept on a tight leash for so long finally exploded. 'You will do no such thing!' he blazed. 'You will do as you are told as the rest of the expedition do! You will remain here!'

'I will go!' she flared, forgetting the good manners she had determined to display. 'I am *not* a member of your expedition, Mr Beauvais. I will do as I please!'

Mark Lane flinched as Raoul blasphemed viciously in French. Harriet, with no knowledge of the language, remained steadfastly on her mount, glaring at him defiantly.

Raoul steeled himself from leaping to the ground, seizing hold of her and shaking her until she begged for mercy. Only the presence of Mark Lane restrained him. With enormous self-control he said through clenched teeth,

'Chief Latika could be a head hunter for all I know.'

'He is an Obbo,' Harriet snapped. 'Wilfred told me so yesterday evening.'

Raoul slammed the fist of one hand into the palm of the other. 'Obbos, head hunters, angels from heaven. Whatever they are, you are not leaving the safety of this camp!'

'I doubt if this camp is any safer than the *dahabiah*,' Harriet retorted, looking pointedly to where Narinda stood, hands clasped and her head bent so that no one could see the secret smile that hovered at the corners of her mouth. 'I am going to the village. If my sketches are to have any value they must depict the lives of the natives we meet on our journeys.'

'That's true,' Wilfred Frome agreed nervously, offering unexpected assistance. 'Miss Latimer's drawings are remarkably good and the Geographical Society will be most grateful for them.'

'Perhaps the Society will be most grateful for Miss Latimer as well, for I am not,' Raoul said cruelly.

It took all of her courage to remain mounted and not to flee from his savage onslaught. 'I go with you,' she repeated, her face white and an under-lying tremble replacing the anger in her voice.

'You can go to the Deuce!' he said explosively and, ignoring the shocked faces of his companions, he dug his heels in his horse's flanks and began to gallop headlong through the knee-high grass in the direction of the village.

'If we were anywhere else I'd call him out for such behaviour,' Sebastian said, his eyes hot with rage.

'Then remember where we are,' Mark Lane said drily. 'Quarrels between ourselves will only destroy our expedition.'

He urged his horse forward and, silently, Harriet riding between them, they cantered at a brisk pace after Raoul's rapidly disappearing figure.

Tall, dry grass brushed their legs. Insects whirred and buzzed and there came the unmistakable roar of a lion. As they approached the compound of straw-thatched dwellings a horde of hungry dogs yapped at their heels and half-naked women and children appeared in curious groups. The drums that had struck fear into her heart the previous day began once more to beat; this time their nearness adding extra menace.

'Do you think they *are* head hunters?' she asked Sebastian nervously as from every direction unsmiling warriors closed in on them, their strong muscled bodies clad only in dusty loincloths, long spears in their hands.

'We'll soon find out,' Sebastian said grimly as they were hemmed in on all sides. 'Where the devil is Beauvais?'

The jostling warriors led them to the centre of the village where, on an enormous platform built of palm trunks and floored with reeds, Raoul and Chief Latika sat cross-legged on leopard-skins, facing each other.

Cautiously Sebastian and Mark dismounted and helped Harriet from her horse. The drums continued to beat as they were led up rough-hewn steps on to the platform, and seated on less prestigious ox skins.

The Chief's eyes flicked over the men and rested on the woman between them. His visitor had been right in what she had said and shown him. The white woman would bring a high price as a slave. Many chiefs, perhaps even King Kamrasi himself, would want to own her. She would bring him many cattle. If the fire in his own loins had not died several years ago, he would have kept her for himself. As to what he had been shown, his fingers tightened around the lock of golden hair. Truly it shone like the sun. Chief Latika smiled, raised his hand to silence the drums and greeted his guest. Raoul spoke to him in a dialect that was-in-comprehensible to his companions but carried overtones of Arabic and was accompanied by much gesticulating. At last Raoul turned to them and said with a fiendish gleam in his eyes,

'Chief Latika wishes us to eat with him.'

Sebastian blanched.

Raoul's white teeth flashed in a grin of pure joy at his dismay. 'Come on, Crale. Join in the hospitality.'

A huge cauldron was carried on the shoulders of several warriors and set in their midst. The smell coming from it was revolting. Mark Lane eased a finger around the inside of his clerical collar and mopped his brow. Sebastian looked decidedly ill. Only Harriet remained outwardly composed.

Clay dishes were filled with the contents of the pot. Raoul began to eat with his fingers, expressing relish for the benefit of his host. Harriet gazed at the mess in her pot and raised her head. A pair of narrow eyes in a lean, dark face watched her with malicious amusement. She scooped the unspeakable concoction into her fingers and ate, her eyes defiant.

'Chief Latika welcomes us,' Raoul said as Sebastian gagged on what appeared to be a chicken feather. 'He offers us bananas and sugar cane and sweet potatoes.'

'Jolly decent of him,' Sebastian said manfully.

Drink, as revolting as the food, was passed around. The drums began to beat again and warrior after warrior spun on to the mud-beaten ground below them, dancing frenziedly. When bare-breasted women also began to dance with immodest vigour, Mark Lane said to Raoul in a hoarse voice,

'How much longer do we have to stay?'

Raoul's mouth quirked in a genuine smile. His clerical companion was the only member of his party of any worth. 'Only until honour is satisfied. To leave too soon would cause offence.'

Mark Lane manfully averted his eyes from the scores of bobbing breasts and breathed a sigh of relief as Latika rose to bid them goodbye.

The platform that had been empty save for themselves was now rapidly filled with perspiring warriors. The drums still beat but they no longer danced, their spears were once more in their hands but they were smiling broadly. Sebastian relaxed. It was nearly over. He had not disgraced himself as Frome had by displaying his reluctance for such an encounter.

Descending the platform was far harder than ascending had been. They were pressed in on all sides by gleaming, foetid bodies. Latika was ahead of them, Raoul at his side, his dark head scarcely visible as he was cut off by a mass of warriors.

Mark Lane's hand reached out to steady Harriet and then he cried out in pain, his face contorted as his arms were wrenched behind his back, and a dozen warriors surged between them. Harriet screamed and fought to free herself of the hands that seized her. Between the milling heads she saw Raoul swing round, saw the flash of comprehension on his face and then she could think no further than that she was about to be trampled to death.

The drums reached crescendo pitch. A thong was slipped over her wrists and she was hauled, kicking and screaming like a captive animal, to where Chief Latika stood, a smile of satisfaction on his face, a cloak of animal skins falling from his shoulders to the ground.

Raoul was at his side, his hand on his pistol, a score of warriors surrounding him, spears at his throat.

Sebastian and Mark Lane were held only feet away, their heads wrenched back, knife blades indenting the skin against their jugular veins.

The shouting and clamour ceased as Harriet was thrown before Chief Latika.

Raoul began to speak angrily and urgently. The Chief answered good-naturedly and reached a large hand towards Harriet. She shrank away, but the gnarled fingers touched the pins at the nape of her neck and tugged them free. A buzz of wonderment arose as Harriet's pale gold hair cascaded in a shining mass, waist-long.

Harriet no longer struggled. She remained still, her eyes fixed on Raoul's desperate face. Sweat had broken out on his forehead. He looked like a man demented as he yelled an unmistakable 'No' to Latika. The elderly chief shrugged.

'For the love of God,' Sebastian choked, 'what does the old devil want?'

Raoul's eyes never left Harriet.

'He wants Harriet,' he said in a voice that was scarcely recognisable. 'He wants to sell her as a slave to one of the neighbouring chiefs.'

Harriet fought to remain conscious. Raoul's eyes burned into hers. All around them the warriors had begun to dance again, the noise deafening.

Sebastian tried to speak, but the knives cut into his flesh and a trickle of blood ran down his throat, scattering scarlet droplets on to his shirt.

'What will happen to you?' Harriet gasped. 'Will he kill you? Will he kill Sebastian and Reverend Lane?'

Raoul's mouth twisted in a mockery of a smile. 'If Latika is to be believed, we are still friends and will be set free – if we leave you behind.'

The blood pounded in her ears. Her heart felt as if it would burst with fear. Her legs would no longer support her and without the cruel hands holding her she would have fallen.

'What will you do?' she whispered through parched lips.

For a long moment their eyes held and then he said tersely, 'Shoot you.' She cried out and fell, only to be hauled back to her feet by a horde of hands.

Raoul's voice throbbed. 'I have only one shot before being speared. If I shoot Latika your fate will be unaltered. There is no alternative.'

'But if you shoot me you will all die! You, and Sebastian and Mark!' She saw his finger tighten on the trigger and knew in a second it would be upraised and that because of her he would sign his own death warrant.

'No!' she cried and trembling like a leaf in the wind she faced Chief Latika.

'Free my companions,' she said with a sob. 'Free them and sell me.'

The chief grinned, understanding her meaning if not her words.

The veins stood out in knots at Raoul's neck and throat. There was one other way, but if it failed they would all be dead men and he would have no weapon with which to end Harriet's life and save her from a far worse fate.

He spoke to Latika rapidly and the Chief nodded, continuing to smile, well pleased with the turn of events. In a world of nightmare Harriet saw Raoul hand Latika his pistol, saw that Sebastian's and Reverend Lane's pistols had already been taken. Saw the ring of spears lower, moving their dreadful points away from Raoul's throat. Saw Raoul move forwards and not backwards. Forward with Chief Latika at his side.

'What is it? What is happening?' she cried fearfully. 'Has he not kept his promise? Are you not free?'

He nodded, his eyes tortured. 'I am free and I am staying.'

'But why?' Her voice was a pant of anguish.

'Because I intend to buy you,' he said and walked with Latika through a mass of warriors who hastily made way for them.

She cried out, but her cries were lost amid the roar and the clamour. She tried to reach him but a swarm of shouting warriors divided them and then she could see him no more. She was seized and as she fought for breath and consciousness she was herded through a mass of glistening, sweating bodies and hurled into darkness.

The pain in her chest was like a knife-wound. She pressed a hand against her heart as if to ease its frenzied beating. She was on her knees on mud-beaten ground. She raised her head. Above her, glimmers of light tried to penetrate the tight thatch of cane and reeds. She was alone in a hut surrounded by hundreds of armed and chanting natives.

And Raoul? Where was Raoul? She leaned back on her heels and tried to conquer her crippling fear with coherent thought. He was only yards away from her. Somewhere, beyond the darkness of the hut into which she had been thrown, he was sitting in friendship with Chief Latika. He was going to save her. He was going to buy her.

The thought sent her springing to her feet and running to the circular walls, searching feverishly with her fingers for a doorway, an opening – anything that would offer her escape. She had entered the village as a free woman. She would leave as one. She would be bought by no man! She would die first!

Her tiny hands hammered against the stout palm trunks, tears streaming down her face. Why had he not shot her? Why had he left her to such a fate? Her nails were broken and bleeding. She could find no doorway and as she covered her face with her hands she knew that even if she had done so, escape would have been impossible. The ground shook with the beating of native feet. The shouting and chanting intensified. Chief Latika was celebrating his new acquisition. She was as captive as the Africans she had seen in the slave markets of Khartoum. Fear could no longer be held at bay. It swept over her in great waves and the name she cried out, time and time again, was not Sebastian's or Mark Lane's – it was Raoul's.

He sat once more on the great ceremonial platform with Chief Latika, a terrified Sebastian and a white-faced Mark Lane at his side. They were not to be allowed back to their camp: not until the neighbouring chiefs had arrived in answer to the summons sent on drums. Not until the white woman had brought Latika great riches.

'Will Frome help us?' Mark Lane whispered frantically to Raoul as Chief Latika's attention was momentarily diverted from his guests.

'No,' Raoul retorted tersely. 'He hasn't the courage, and even if he had, there is no way he could save Harriet except by shooting her.'

Sebastian wiped the sweat from his brow with a trembling hand. 'Will the old devil keep his word? Will he free us after . . . After . . .?' He faltered, unable to meet the contempt in Raoul's fiery eyes.

'After Harriet has been sold, body and soul? Yes Crale. No doubt Latika will keep his word and free you.' The savagery in his voice made Sebastian wince. 'But only if my gamble pays off and I am the purchaser. If I am outbid . . .' He paused, unable to continue, his mouth twisted in pain and anguish.

'If you are outbid, what will you do?' Mark Lane prompted quietly.

'Kill her,' he said, his eyes no longer seeing the gloating face of Latika or the swarms of warriors. He could see only Harriet, golden-haired and trembling, offering herself freely to Latika in the mistaken belief that to do so would set himself and his companions free. She had more courage in her slender body than Frome and Crale had in their little fingers.

He had known he loved her before he had left Khartoum. His decision had been made even then. He had told Hashim and he had told Narinda he was going to marry the English girl he had brought into the city. The prospect had amazed even himself. Marriage had never before been a prerequisite for love-making. Previous affairs had been enjoyed without the least notion of satisfying the lady's honour. His reputation was notorious. The most astute gamblers in Cairo and Alexandria would have staked their all against Raoul Beauvais ever marrying. Yet he had been on the verge of doing so. It was Harriet herself who had deflected him, displaying coolness and indifference where she had previously displayed passion and a spirit as adventurous as his own.

His frown deepened so that his winged brows met and even Chief Latika did not intrude on his private thoughts.

What had happened in Khartoum? What had changed? When she had ridden after them he had been beside himself with jealousy, believing that she had done so to be with Sebastian Crale. Yet watching them covertly, day after day, he had known that whatever Crale had believed, it was not so. She was no more in love with Crale than she was with him. She wanted one thing and one thing alone: to stand at the fountains of the Niles and enter the history books of the world.

He groaned. She would never do so now. She would die here, in a nameless native village, and no one would ever know of her bravery.

'How will you kill her?' Mark Lane asked desperately. 'We have no weapons, no pistols.'

'I shall kill her,' Raoul replied with a quiet ferocity that silenced his friend. He would seize a spear from the nearest hand and throw it at her heart. He would kill her because he loved her more than life itself. Her death would mean his own death and the death of Mark Lane and Sebastian Crale. There was no alternative.

Mark Lane, understanding, stilled a momentary terror and then regained control of himself. He had only one way of helping to alleviate Harriet's distress, and that was by praying. He closed his eyes and prayed in silent intensity.

All through the long night Raoul's tortured eyes never left the circular hut into which Harriet had been thrown. It was so well guarded that a battalion of men would have had difficulty in storming it. Certainly there was no opportunity for overcoming his own guard and retrieving his pistol.

Slowly the hours passed and dawn approached. No food or water was taken into the hut. He wondered if she was bound or free and felt himself to be in an inner hell. He had no way of speaking with her; no way of explaining his actions. He could imagine the gold-green eyes that sparkled so easily with fury or laughter, widening in terror as he raised the spear. There would be no last word; no last caress. Her scream would be the only sound he would carry to his grave.

Sleepless, every nerve and muscle in his body taut, he faced Latika the next day with outward ease. One hint of fear and Latika's friendship would deteriorate into contempt and he would not be treated as an equal and allowed to bid for Harriet alongside the arriving chiefs.

They sat in splendour beside Latika; big men dressed in brilliantly-coloured togas with cloaks of leopard skins around their shoulders and retinues of warriors about their heels. As the sun rose higher in the sky, Latika motioned for Raoul to join them on the ceremonial platform. Below, wedged in with the jostling throng of hundreds of warriors and wives, and squalling children, Mark Lane and Sebastian Crale watched fearfully.

Strong sunlight flooded into the darkened hut as the door was flung open and two warriors entered. Momentarily blinded, Harriet lashed out vainly at them, but weakened and exhausted, her blows had no effect. Her arms were wrenched behind her back, the leather thong slipped over her wrists as she was led stumbling into the heat and dust.

Every fibre of Raoul's being cried out in revolt. The muscles in his neck and shoulders stood out in knots as he fought to keep his iron control. One false move now, and they would all be destroyed. He would have to suffer the ordeal as she was suffering it. He saw her chin tilt defiantly upwards, saw the slender shoulders square and knew that when she faced Latika and his fellow chiefs there would be no fear in her eyes. It was a satisfaction she would not give them.

Robbed of its pin, her hair streamed down her back in all its glory, the sun's rays glinting on it so that it looked like gold. Climbing the rough-hewn steps to the platform it fell forward and with her hands bound she could not push it back from her face. She swung her head in an attempt to do so and it swirled in a silken cloud.

Around him Raoul could hear the chiefs draw in their breath

and he clenched his jaws. What could he offer Latika in competition with the men at his side? He had only his horse and pack animals; his stores and equipment. Would such possessions be of worth to Latika? It was impossible for him to tell. What was obvious was that the chiefs around him would pay a high price in whatever currency Latika demanded to possess the beautiful woman with hair like the sun.

Harriet's eyes sought Raoul's. Latika was speaking to him and Raoul was smiling, sitting cross-legged on the leopard skins, as at ease as if he were in Khartoum. She choked back a sob. She had thought he had stayed to try and save her, that his agony of mind had been as great as hers. She had been wrong. He was staying because Latika had declared himself to be his friend. Because he could hardly abandon her in front of Sebastian and Mark Lane without making a token effort to save her life.

He raised his head from Latika's and she tore her eyes away, staring steadfastly ahead of her, her heart hammering like a caged bird. She would retain her inner dignity at all costs, no matter how publicly she was humiliated. She would remember who she was. What she was. Harriet Latimer, missionary's daughter.

A heavy-muscled body with many ankle bracelets stepped towards her and she closed her eyes as she felt the sweat of his body and his hands touching her hair, her chin imprisoned between strong fingers and turned from left to right.

She would think of Cheltenham; of her aunts; of sweet, rain-washed mornings and fragrant spring days.

She felt exposed to the whole world. Before her were the chiefs and their retinues, and Raoul. Behind her hundreds of others and somewhere, if they were still alive, Sebastian and Mark Lane.

Her body was touched as if she were a horse or a mare about to be sold. She remembered how the slaves in Khartoum had been made to walk and run for the benefit of their prospective masters. She remained motionless, her eyes closed, transporting herself mentally far from her tortured body as it was discussed, fingered, bartered for.

She remembered her father, his gentleness and kindness, his love for her. The drums had begun to pound again. Voices were raised in excitement and anger. Flies buzzed around her and the blazing sun beat down on her unprotected head so that it required all of her strength to remain upright. She had lost count of the hours she had been without water. Her mouth was parched, her lips cracked. She could hear Raoul's voice, deep and strong and totally self-assured. Her eyelids flickered open. She knew she was going to faint. That when she regained consciousness she would belong to one of the impassive-faced chiefs standing only feet away from her; that Raoul and Sebastian and Mark Lane would be safe and continuing with their expedition. That she would never see him again. He had abandoned her, had witnessed her humiliation and had not raised his voice in protest.

It was hard for her to focus. Colours and shapes shifted and slid. It seemed as if the grass-coloured platform was full of objects that had not been there previously. Objects that were familiar. She swayed and closed her eyes and opened them again. There were sextants and chronometers, telescopes and beads. The chief was rifling through crates that she had last seen in camp. Raoul was showing him how to use the telescope and the chief was crowing with delight.

Why did Raoul not look at her? Why did he not care? Was he there at all or had she entered a world of fantasy? She looked around dazedly. On the ground behind her the crowd had parted to allow Raoul's horse and Sebastian's and Mark Lane's to be paraded in front of Latika.

Around Latika the other chiefs clustered, whispering, eyeing Raoul malevolently.

Raoul strolled to the edge of the ceremonial platform and called Mark Lane's name. Through a haze she saw Mark's strained face and saw him pull the rifle from Raoul's saddle bag and throw it up to him. Raoul caught it easily and turned to the chief. Immediately there was silence. Every warrior gripped his spear, pointing it in Raoul's direction. Raoul shrugged and smiled and approached Latika.

Latika relaxed slightly as Raoul spoke to him, handing him the gleaming rifle.

Amidst the crowd, Mark Lane closed his eyes. He had forgotten the rifle. He knew that Raoul had forgotten it also until he had seen it still in his pack when the horses had been paraded. Mark had believed that in the instant he had thrown it up to Raoul he would have been a dead man. Throughout the night the pistols that had been taken from them had been used with childlike glee and now Raoul was giving Latika their only remaining weapon. Mark wondered if the events of the past twenty-four hours had unhinged his mind.

The chief grinned and kept hold of the rifle. Raoul continued to talk. The chief looked disbelieving. The warrior who proudly disported Sebastian's pistol was summoned from the crowd.

Raoul stood before him, legs apart, arms folded over his powerful chest. The warrior raised the pistol and pulled the trigger. Harriet screamed and fell to her knees. Mark Lane groaned and closed his eyes. Sebastian cried out for his Maker, knowing that with Raoul dead they were all doomed.

Raoul gave silent thanks that his maths had been correct and held out his hand for the pistol. Latika was on his feet, frowning. The two other pistols were brought. They would not make the terrible noise they made when they had first been seized.

Harriet lay limply on the grass and reeds. She had thought him dead but he was still before her, talking to Latika. The chief's eyes were narrow and sharp. He raised the rifle and at Raoul's direction aimed it in the air and fired. His warriors cheered wildly. Latika beamed. He raised the rifle and fired again. Nothing happened. Latika frowned. Then Raoul showed him how to reload it. The bullets would not fit the pistols. Only the chief's weapon could make a voice like thunder and shoot the birds from the air. Latika was buoyant. The chiefs and their offers of cattle and wives were dismissed.

Raoul was striding towards her, his face grim. She tried to speak and could not. In one swift movement he swept her into his arms and then, in a semi-conscious haze, she knew they were descending the wooden steps. She saw Sebastian and Mark's frightened faces, felt herself lifted into the saddle in front of Raoul, held in the crook of his arm as she had been on the journey to Khartoum. Past and present merged into one. Her eyes were open but she no longer saw. She spoke to her father, her aunts, Dr Walther. She was vaguely aware of being tended; of being lifted to the ground and being given water to drink. Of her brow being sponged.

Raoul's voice penetrated her consciousness but it was hard and demanding and she knew that he still did not love her and wondered who was treating her with such tenderness.

He would allow no one to go near her. Holding her in his arms he tersely informed Frome what had happened and rallied Sebastian and Mark from their terrified stupor. The chief had been so elated with the rifle that fired only for him that they had been allowed to leave with their horses and most of their instruments, though not with Wilfred Frome's telescope. Latika's elation would not last longer than the ammunition that had been left with him. Their only hope of safety lay in removing themselves with all speed from the area inhabited by him and his fellow chiefs.

Sebastian was in eager agreement but wished to retrace his steps, not go forward. Mark Lane, when asked bluntly by Raoul whether he wanted to continue or return, had said that he personally wished to continue but that Harriet was in no condition to do so and would need protection. Looking down at Harriet's fevered brow, Raoul knew that his expedition was over and did not care. All that mattered was that Harriet was safe and would remain safe. He gave Mark Lane the double-barrelled Fletcher that he had once given to Harriet but that she had never carried, and asked him to take turns standing guard with Wilfred Frome. They would ride at dawn after Harriet had rested.

Then, caring nothing for the proprieties, he ignored Sebastian's suggestion that Narinda nurse her through the night hours, and carried her into her tent, kneeling at her side, tending her as gently as if she were a child.

'Papa!' she called out several times, clinging to him, relaxing as she felt the strength and safety of his arms. And then, as dawn flushed the sky blood red, she said wonderingly, 'Raoul,' and he breathed a shuddering sigh of relief and clasped her tightly to his chest.

Tentatively she raised her hand, her fingers outlining the hard contours of his face. 'Raoul,' she breathed softly. 'Raoul,' and his dark eyes held hers and he was kissing her long and lingeringly and with increasing passion.

Her arms slid up and around his neck. She wanted nothing more than to lose herself in the sweetness of his mouth, to yield utterly. To feel the warmth of his body against hers. Where were they? In Berber? In Khartoum? Her head whirled, besieged by faces and images.

The slave market in Khartoum. Sebastian's voice saying idly, as he sipped his wine, 'Beauvais has only one mistress, the Circassian, Narinda.'

Raoul's hand clasping Narinda's. Narinda kneeling at his feet, sewing his shirts, and then the floodgates of memory were opened and she was once again standing like a chattel before Latika and Raoul and she was being bought; bought as Narinda had been bought. Bought by Raoul Beauvais as his slave.

Her forehead burned. She was consumed with a fire that was destroying her. His lips seared hers and she wrenched her head away, drumming her fists against his chest and shoulders, crying, 'Don't touch me! Don't touch me! Don't ever touch me!'

Raoul raised his head from hers, as sharply as if he had been shot. She twisted in his arms, calling out vainly 'Sebastian!'

Raoul ground his teeth and tightened his hold on her so that her cry became one of pain.

'Sebastian is it? What did your precious Sebastian do for you in Latika's village? Did he risk his life for you? Did he carry you to safety?'

She was no longer listening to him. She knew only that she must free herself from his hold; that she must regain her self-respect. Her nails dug into his cheeks, raking long scratchmarks.

'I'm not Narinda!' she cried tormentedly. 'I'm not a slave to be taken at your pleasure!'

The blood pounded in a red mist behind his eyes. He had ached for her body for months. He had risked his life for her and now that she was safe it was Crale's name she called out. His iron self-control snapped. His fingers twisted cruelly in her hair, pulling her head back so that his eyes blazed into hers.

'You *are* a slave!' he yelled as she panted and struggled and tried to free herself. 'Ask Chief Latika! Ask his hundreds of warriors! Ask Crale and Lane! You were auctioned as a slave and bought as a slave and by God I'll enjoy you as one!'

This time there was no tenderness in the mouth that bruised hers. His body pinned her to the ground, no longer a refuge but hard and threatening and terrifyingly arousing. She could feel the heavy thud of his heart against her breast, and the passion that she had fought for so long engulfed her. She was on fire, burning with a need that knew no bounds. His lips scalded hers, hurting, searching, demanding. From the depths of her soul she summoned up one last agonised protest and as the word 'No' was torn from her body the tent flaps were ripped apart and violent hands seized hold of Raoul.

She rolled from beneath him, gasping and sobbing, overcome with shame at her weakness.

Raoul had twisted like an eel, his fist coming into contact with the first face he saw. It was Sebastian's and he went spinning backwards out of the tent and into the dust and dirt. Seconds later, Raoul and Wilfred and Mark Lane followed him.

In two swift movements Raoul reduced Wilfred Frome to retching inertness and only a blow from Mark Lane, still wearing his clerical collar, brought him to his senses. They stood facing each other, panting, fists clenched.

'Don't be a fool, Raoul. I don't want to hit you,' Mark gasped.

Raoul laughed harshly. 'If you do, I'll knock you unconscious.'

'If that's what I have to suffer to have you come to your senses, then I will.'

Raoul stared at him long and hard and then swore, swinging on his heel, half running in his haste to be free of the camp. Free of Mark Lane's accusing eyes. Free of Harriet's tormenting presence.

Mark rasped for breath and wiped a trickle of blood away from his mouth.

'Is he sane?' Wilfred asked, staggering to his feet. 'Will he be back?'

'He's sane and he'll be back,' Mark Lane said and went to where Harriet stood, Sebastian's arm comfortingly around her shoulders, her eyes huge in her whitened face.

'You mustn't think too badly of Raoul,' Mark said, still fighting for breath. 'He's been through a hellish experience . . .'

'We all have,' Sebastian interrupted curtly.

Mark's voice was sharp. 'It was Raoul who bore the brunt of it.'

'Please don't apologise for him,' Harriet said, choking back her tears. 'He is beyond apology.'

'Frome and I are returning to Gondokoro at dawn,' Sebastian said tersely. 'Miss Latimer will be accompanying us. For your information, her reputation will be untarnished. She has just done me the honour of accepting my proposal of marriage.'

'Is that true?' Mark stared at Harriet, deeply shocked.

Harriet's eyes met his bleakly. 'Yes,' she said with an underlying tremble in her voice. 'It's quite true,' and then she turned and stepped into her tent, letting the flaps fall behind her.

Chapter Ten

Narinda's eyes were triumphant. Ignoring Wilfred's half-hearted protests, she ran towards her mule and mounted, urging the animal in the direction Raoul had taken.

Sebastian approached Harriet's tent, standing awkwardly as he heard the distinct sound of weeping.

'Strange behaviour for a happy bride-to-be,' Wilfred Frome said nastily as he returned to his own tent.

Sebastian stepped towards him threateningly. 'I find my fiancee's behaviour perfectly understandable in the given circumstances. I intend leaving this camp before she has to see that fiend again.'

'If and when we part company, it will be in an orderly manner,' Mark Lane said quietly.

'It will be when I choose!' Sebastian snapped, turning on his heel, unable to summon enough courage to comfort his betrothed.

Harriet wept until she could weep no more. In the long hours of captivity in the native hut she had been forced to face an agonising truth. No matter what he did, no matter how despicable his behaviour, she would always love Raoul Beauvais. She could do nothing else. He had only to touch her for her blood to leap. Even when he had hurt her, wrenching her head back, kissing her with a savagery that had left her lips bleeding, she had responded. Her last protest in his arms had been a vain one. Only Sebastian and his companions had saved her from utter shamelessness. She moaned softly, covering her eyes with her arm. What had she done that she should suffer such torments? She had discouraged him, ignored him, refused to be beguiled by his charm as Mark Lane and even Chief Latika had been. And to what avail? She was still enslaved by him. Nothing she could do would free her from the folly of her own heart.

Desolation swept over her. How would she live without the pleasure of seeing him? Without hearing his deep, rich voice? Without being the recipient of his rare smiles, his murderous rages? How would she live without the man she loved most in the world?

She raised herself and pulled back the flap of the tent. Outside the moon burned amongst a cloud of stars. She could see the dark silhouette of Mark Lane as he kept vigilant watch, her Fletcher in his hands. She wondered if Raoul had returned and knew that he had not.

She let the flap fall and lay down once again. Tomorrow their ways would diverge. She would return to Khartoum with Wilfred and Sebastian and the Africa she had loved would be lost to her. Without Raoul it would be meaningless.

In the early hours of dawn she heard the thud of the mule's hooves and Narinda's soft laugh as Raoul spoke tersely to Mark Lane. She began to braid her hair with trembling hands. The night had not been lonely for him. She doubted if he had spent one moment of it thinking of her. He would say goodbye to her as easily as he would to Sebastian or Wilfred. She paused for a few moments before emerging from the tent, steeling herself so that her outward appearance was composed. She took a deep, shuddering breath, clasped her hands close together and stepped out into the beauty of the dawn.

The lines around his mouth were white and strained, his eyes disbelieving as he listened to Mark Lane. He swung in her direction his barely-controlled fury rooting her to the spot.

'Are you to marry Crale?' The question was like a lash.

She flinched visibly and saw Mark Lane rest a restraining hand on his arm.

'Yes.' Her eyes held his bravely, but her voice was barely audible.

'Leave my fiancée alone, Beauvais,' Sebastian said threateningly, walking towards them, Wilfred Frome's pistol at his hip, his hand resting on the stock.

Raoul's eyes burned into hers, dark pits in which she could read nothing.

'We are packed and ready to leave,' Sebastian continued tightly. 'Frome is travelling with us and so are most of the bearers.'

At last, when she felt unable to bear it for another second, he tore his eyes from hers and said tersely to Mark Lane, 'I am continuing. The choice is yours.'

'I travel with you.'

Raoul nodded briefly and ignored both Sebastian and Harriet, speaking to Wilfred.

'Narinda will travel back with you. The dangers ahead are too great.'

'No!' Narinda's protest was a shriek. She threw herself at Raoul, flinging her arms around his neck, tears pouring down her face.

Harriet turned away. For the first time she felt a measure of compassion for the lovely native girl. Her use had come to an end and so she was being discarded – as she herself had been.

The shrieks and sobs continued until the horses had been packed and no trace of their campsite remained.

There were no handshakes on parting. Sebastian merely nodded curtly in Raoul and Mark's direction, and Wilfred muttered an awkward farewell. Narinda, her pleas and tears to no avail, continued to weep, her face ravaged with grief.

Harriet felt as if the breath were being squeezed from her body. She sat on her horse, her hands clasped so tightly together that the nail marks indented her skin. Every fibre of her being yearned to do as Narinda had done; to hurl herself from the saddle and race across to him, throwing herself at his feet and begging to be taken with him. Her eyes were tortured. She could well imagine his contempt if she did so.

She sat proudly, her back straight and her head erect. Her world had come to an end but none would know it had done so.

Sebastian flicked his horse into movement. Behind her, Wilfred's horse nudged hers impatiently. Her horse began to move. She was leaving him. She would never see him again.

'Harriet!' Her name was torn from his throat.

The horses broke into a canter; he called again, running with panther-like speed, seizing hold of her reins.

'Harriet!'

She closed her eyes, her face bloodless. For one brief moment his hand rested on hers. 'Goodbye, *ma chérie*,' he said, and then Sebastian was slapping the flank of her horse and goading it to a gallop and she could not reply for the unshed tears that choked her throat.

'Damned insolence,' Sebastian said viciously as Raoul was left standing in the wake of their galloping horses.

When she turned in the saddle she could no longer see him. Perhaps one day she would read of his return or of his death. She was oblivious of the heat; oblivious of the conversation taking place between Wilfred and Sebastian; oblivious of Narinda's tears.

She was lost in a world of such unhappiness that it seemed impossible that she could survive it. His touch still burned on the back of her hand. She raised it to her cheek and pressed it there, travelling mile after mile and seeing nothing but his face and the dark, unreadable depths of his eyes.

Several of the native bearers who had elected to return had eyed Sebastian and Wilfred uneasily and had melted away so that when they made camp they found that they had only half the number they had started out with.

'Treacherous dogs,' Sebastian said, his voice edged with fear. He had never been in the position of leader before and it was not one he was relishing.

'Raoul and Mark will be grateful for them,' Harriet said quietly.

'What the devil is it to you whether Beauvais is grateful for them or not?' Sebastian snapped, the back of his neck prickling as a distant beast roared with hunger.

'I want his expedition to succeed,' she replied simply.

Wilfred Frome laughed. 'How can it succeed? They are without a weapon between them.'

'They will succeed,' Harriet insisted with quiet conviction, building a campfire as Sebastian, Wilfred and Narinda watched without offering assistance.

'They'll never be heard of again,' Sebastian said with satisfaction. 'Wilfred will inform the Geographical Society of Beauvais' infamous conduct and lack of leadership and Wilfred and I will lead another expedition; better equipped and better informed. After we are married,' he added as an afterthought.

The flames of the fire took hold and Harriet rose to her feet and faced him. 'I am sorry, Sebastian. I should never have accepted your proposal of marriage. I did so in the same way it was offered – in a moment of extreme stress. I would be grateful if we did not discuss the subject again.'

Sebastian's mouth tightened. He was about to argue with her but the roving beast roared again and this time there was no mistaking the sound.

'Lion,' Wilfred said, paling.

The two men looked at each other. 'The fire will keep it away,' Sebastian said nervously.

'One of us should go after him.'

'You have the pistol.'

'You are the hunter.'

Sweat broke out on Sebastian's brow and Wilfred shifted uncomfortably from one foot to another.

'You may take my Fletcher,' Harriet said to Sebastian and was rewarded with a look of such venom that it startled her.

Wilfred went for the Fletcher eagerly and handed it to an ungrateful Sebastian.

Sebastian snatched it from his grasp and said savagely, 'You go east of the camp, I'll go north. He's in that vicinity somewhere.'

Unhappily Wilfred did as he was bid and Harriet busied herself searching through their provisions for anything with which to cook an adequate meal.

Without Raoul, the native bearers were uneasy and unhelpful. Narinda sat motionless by the fire, staring into the flames with anguished eyes. Harriet sighed. Without salt she could cook nothing and the salt was in one of the bundles the bearers had carried through the heat of the day on their heads.

She left the crackling fire and the group of natives and began searching for the salt herself. The eerie silence of the African night pressed in on her. The lion no longer roared. There was no sound of hoofbeats.

She found oil and spices but no salt. The bearers had dropped their packs in wild disarray far from where Sebastian had erected the tents. As she stepped further from the flickering light of the campfire and into the impenetrable darkness her skirt caught on an acacia bush. She pulled it free and as she did so a shower of dead locusts scattered over her hand. She shook them off and stared at the black outline of the acacia bush. Scores of dead locusts were impaled on the vicious thorns. Free, they had flown directly on to the bush to a sudden and painful death, just as free she had flown into Raoul's arms, and a lifetime of torment.

The roar and the screams were simultaneous. For a second she could not move and then she was racing back to the campfire and the marauding lion. It stood over Narinda, its tail lashing viciously from side to side; the skin curled back over its dreadful teeth as it seized hold of its vainly struggling victim.

On the far side of the fire Wilfred stared petrified.

'*Shoot it!*' Harriet screamed at him. '*For God's sake, shoot it!*'

Wilfred continued to stare, shaking like a man with the palsy.

Frenziedly Harriet flew to his side and seized his pistol. In doing so she passed within feet of the great beast, attracting its attention. She was uncaring. Narinda was still alive, moaning piteously. The lion dropped her from its jaw and began to pace towards Harriet. Wilfred screamed and fled into the darkness, leaving Harriet to face death alone. She could smell Narinda's blood; smell her own fear. Tawny eyes glowed in the darkness, powerful muscles crouched low, preparing to spring.

Narinda cried out inarticulately, one hand raised supplicatingly in Harriet's direction.

With a great roar the lion sprang from its haunches and Harriet squeezed the trigger.

The momentum of the animal sent her sprawling, its weight suffocating her. She fought against the hot flesh, screaming, gouging, kicking. There was blood on her face, her bodice, her skirt. She was lost in her screams, drowning in them and then Sebastian had hold of her.

'*It's all right! It's dead! Dead!*' He was shaking convulsively.

'Narinda,' she gasped and pushing him away she ran to the native girl's side.

Narinda barely whimpered as Sebastian carried her into the shelter of a tent. All through the long night Harriet tore up her underskirts, bedding: anything at all that could help staunch the flow of blood and all the time Narinda's eyes were on hers and she murmured repeatedly,

'I saw. He ran away but you stayed. I saw. I saw.'

Neither Sebastian nor Harriet spoke to Wilfred when he returned. Unasked, he boiled water continually, burning blood-soaked bandages, assisting in searching for new ones.

'Will she live?' Sebastian asked as dawn tinged the sky with gold.

Harriet shook her head, sponging Narinda's fevered brow, holding her hand.

'I saw.' Narinda said again, her eyelids fluttering open. 'I saw and I am sorry.'

'Don't talk,' Harriet said gently. 'Save your strength.'

Narinda shook her head. Her voice was a whisper but her eyes were urgent. 'I am sorry,' she repeated with great difficulty. 'I hated you and I am sorry.'

Harriet pressed a sponge of drinking water against her lips. 'Please don't talk any more, Narinda. Try and sleep.'

'No!' Her hold on Harriet's hand tightened, her eyes wide. 'You must go to him. He loves you and you must go to him.'

'She is delirious,' Sebastian said shortly.

Harriet paid no heed to him. Her eyes were fixed on Narinda's.

'I knew what you believed,' the native girl gasped, 'that I was his mistress.' Tears filled her lustrous eyes. 'I have never been his mistress. My master cares for me and he is kind but he has never loved me. He never loved anyone.' She faltered, rasping for breath.

Harriet cooled her forehead, her hands trembling as she did so.

Narinda's voice was failing. Harriet had to lean close to hear each desperately summoned word.

'He loves you,' she whispered. 'He told me so in Khartoum. He told Hashim so. He said . . .' She panted harshly. 'He said that he was going to marry you.'

A long, deep breath escaped from Harriet's lips.

'I was glad when you refused him. When you thought that I . . . that I . . .'

'Hush now, Narinda, there is no need to say any more.'

'You will go to him?'

'Yes, I will go to him.'

A smile touched Narinda's lips. 'I am sorry,' she said again and died.

There was a long silence. Harriet leaned back on her heels, Narinda's hand still in hers. At last Sebastian said awkwardly,

'She didn't know what she was saying.'

'She knew perfectly what she was saying. She made only one mistake. Raoul may have intended asking to marry me but he never did so. If he had I would never have refused him, Narinda or no Narinda.' Slowly she rose to her feet and stepped out of the tent, into the morning sunlight.

Sebastian followed her, standing at her side. 'What are you going to do?' he asked, his face troubled.

'I am going to do as Narinda said. I am going to go to him.'

Sebastian's face, so attractive in Khartoum, had aged prematurely in the last few days. Fresh anxiety swept across it.

'You can't! It would be suicide for us to return to Latika's lands.'

'I am returning,' she repeated quietly. 'I will join Raoul and if that means crossing Latika's lands, then I will do so.'

'I can't . . . won't . . .' Sebastian floundered incoherently.

She smiled up at him. 'I don't expect an escort, Sebastian. You and Wilfred return to Khartoum. I shall journey to Raoul alone. It is only a day since we parted. I shall find him and then I shall never leave him.'

Hurriedly she packed a small supply of rations in her saddlebag.

'But if you die . . .' Sebastian protested weakly.

Her smile widened, a radiant smile of pure happiness.

'My life is my own, Sebastian. I shall do with it what I will.'

He kissed her goodbye on the cheek and she shook a shame-faced Wilfred by the hand.

He was a coward and she had been a fool. She had paid for her folly and no doubt Wilfred would pay for his cowardice. She preferred her own failing to his. It was one that would not assail her again.

She felt as free as a caged bird that had suddenly been given the whole sky to fly in and, like a bird, her heart sang as she galloped away from the two watching men and into the great, vast wilderness that was Africa.

Ahead of her lay a continent still unexplored, and a man she loved with all her heart. Despair had turned to hope and hope to certainty. There would be no more foolish pride. She was his and he was hers. She had only to tell him so.

She rode hard and confidently and when she camped alone at night she did so without fear. Another day, two at the most, and she would be once more at his side. Her small campfire flickered bravely in the velvety blackness. She sat close to it, her arms hugging her knees. Her unhappiness had been of her own making. She had shown neither compassion nor understanding. Though Narinda had not been able to tell her, she knew now why Raoul had brought her and treated her with the same courtesy he would have a European. It was because, in his eyes, the natives and Europeans were equal and demanded equal respect. It was how he treated Hashim; how he treated all who came into contact with him unless they violated his own code of honour as the Pasha had done.

Kindness had prompted him to buy Narinda and save her from a life of degradation. Kindness had prompted him to care for her. It had been a kindness totally misunderstood in Khartoum. She could imagine his contempt for those who thought his motives base. As she had done. Her cheeks flushed. She had not deserved his love in those far off days in Khartoum. She had been immature and naive. She was neither now.

At dawn she rode again and at dusk she camped alone. She had food for another two days' travel. She knew only that he was journeying south. She should have been in fear of her life and instead she was filled with the calm certainty that he was only a little way ahead of her.

On the third day, as the sun sank in a blood-red haze, she climbed a hill and saw two distant figures below her on the ochre plain. They had resumed contact with the Nile. It flowed between grassy banks and dense foliage and as she watched, the two men entered a grove of trees and disappeared from her view.

The way down to the plain was steep and treacherous and common sense told her to wait for daylight. Her heart was unable to do so. As darkness gathered she made her way carefully down the hillside, her mount moving with the same sureness that she herself felt. It was night by the time they reached the plain and she set her horse's head in the direction of the river and the trees and urged it to one last gallant effort.

The two men had hardly spoken since separating from the others. Raoul had retreated into a world of bitterness and pain that not even Mark Lane could penetrate. They sat as they had done each evening, Mark Lane reading his Bible, Raoul staring broodingly into the flames of the fire. The ground shook with hoofbeats. Branches rustled and cracked as they were pushed heedlessly aside.

In unison the two men sprang to their feet, grabbing the wooden staves that were their only protection. There was no subtlety, no cunning, in the animal's approach.

'It must be wounded,' Mark Lane hissed as, bodies tensed, they waited for the intruder to burst from the trees.

'Faster, faster,' Harriet gasped as she smelt the smoke from their fire and knew that only yards of darkness separated them. Leaves clung to her face. A snake whipped to safety. With a cry of joy she pushed the last branch aside and galloped into the clearing.

Mark Lane's stave left his hand and sent the terrified horse rearing.

Raoul stood transfixed, unable to believe his eyes. She slithered from her horse's back, laughing and sobbing with relief and happiness.

'I've come back! I love you and I've come back!' she cried, and like an arrow flying into the gold she flew into his outstretched arms.

'Harriet! My sweet love! *Ma chérie!*' His face was alight with naked joy as he pressed kisses on her eyes, her mouth, her throat.

She clung to him as if she would never let him go and only Mark Lane's discreet cough prevented Raoul from sinking to the ground and making violent love to her.

'Your presence is unexpected, but very welcome, Harriet. What occasioned it?' he asked as they remained fervently clasped in each other's arms.

Harriet's breath steadied. She held Raoul's eyes and said simply, 'Narinda died. It was a lion. I'm sorry, Raoul. There was nothing we could do.' She had long since forced to the back of her mind the vision of Wilfred standing motionless, the Fletcher in his hand.

'As she was dying she told me what I should have known all along. That she was not your mistress. That you love me as I love you.'

Raoul groaned and buried his head in her hair. 'Is that what you believed, sweet love?'

Her tears were wet against his cheek. 'Yes, but it should have made no difference to me. It would not now.' She gave a tremulous smile and raised her face to his. 'I was a child then, Raoul. I am a child no longer.'

His breath caught in his throat as he gazed at the beauty of her upturned face. 'I love you, *ma chère petite,*' he said and when his lips met hers it was with the gentleness of absolute love.

Mark Lane cleared his throat, the gravity of his voice belying the laughter in his eyes. 'I'm afraid I can be no party to any irregular relationship.'

Raoul raised his head from Harriet's, his eyes darkening. 'I would not want you to be. We shall marry at the earliest opportunity.' His voice was decisive. 'We shall break camp at dawn and begin our return to Khartoum.'

Harriet's eyes widened, 'But why? There is no need.'

'There is every need,' he said, his dark eyes gleaming. 'I am a man, not a saint. I cannot travel with you at my side and treat you as a sister.'

Her cheeks flushed prettily. 'There is no need,' she said and pressed her lips against his.

Mark Lane shook his head in mock sorrow at such immodesty and said, 'Then if you are both ready, we will begin.'

They turned to him, uncomprehendingly, arms still entwined.

He smiled, his Bible in his hand. 'I am an ordained minister. I believe that is the only necessity required by God in order to sanctify a marriage. That, and two people who love each other.'

Raoul broke a lush-white blossom from the nearby foliage and standing by the nearby campfire, the single blossom in her hair, their only guests wild creatures of the night, Mark Lane married Harriet Latimer to Raoul Beauvais.

They stood gazing at each other, two people in a world of their own.

'You may now kiss the bride,' Mark Lane prompted, a smile tugging at the corners of his mouth.

Raoul's arms circled her waist and he gazed down at the woman he loved and who was now his wife. 'It will be a lonely life and a dangerous one, *chérie.*'

Harriet smiled gently, dismissing the thought of danger. She had faced it many times and would no doubt face it many times again. Danger was becoming quite an old friend. Her eyes were radiant with love as she said softly,

'Our life will never be lonely. Not for as long as we have each other.'

Mark Lane quietly picked up his sleeping bag and moved off into the darkness. The night was theirs and the Lord would watch over his own, solitary sleep.

The flames of the fire leapt and danced, their hiss and crackle the only sound as the dark head bent low to the gold and Raoul Beauvais kissed his bride.

Chapter Eleven

They had travelled for many months. Mark Lane's beard had taken on patriarchal proportions. Harriet's skin was no longer creamy white, but a glowing honey colour that emphasised the beauty of her hair and eyes. Raoul was no longer the brooding, solitary figure he had been for so many years. His laughter rang out loud and often and now, as they faced the hill before them, his eyes were alight with a sense of achievement.

Beyond it lay Luta N'zige. Dead Locust Lake. The lake from which the Nile flowed.

Mark reined in his horse. 'I want to take our bearings. I'll do that and make camp.' His eyes held Raoul's steadily. The friendship between the two men had deepened to such a point that words were no longer necessary between them. Mark was offering him the opportunity of standing at the fountains of the Nile with only Harriet at his side.

With eyes suspiciously bright, Raoul left Mark setting up his chronometer and sextant and with Harriet's horse cantering at his side, crossed the valley floor and climbed up the gently sloping hill that barred any view of the way ahead.

Harriet's heart beat fast and light. Were they at last to see their objective? Were her father's dreams to be made a reality? Was the lake that had been only legend going to prove to be fact?

A short distance from the summit Raoul reined in and dismounted. Feverishly, like two children, they ran the last few yards with clasped hands and crowned the hill. Below them the lake stretched like a sea of silver, crocodiles and hippopotami lying in its shallows, herds of topi and hartebeest grazing on the lush banks. Beyond, in the distance, was the blue haze of mountains.

Harriet sank to her knees on fine, soft grass. 'We've found the Garden of Eden,' she whispered.

Raoul knelt beside her, his arms circling her shoulders. 'We've found the source of the Nile,' he said reverently.

She looked up at him and her eyes were suddenly troubled. 'Once it is known in Europe, hundreds will find their way here.'

'Would that displease you, *mon amour?*' he asked, her soft, sensuous body yielding against his own.

She turned her head, looking once more on the peace and tranquillity that no European had ever before set eyes on.

'Yes,' she said simply, 'it would.'

'Then we shall leave Europe in ignorance until some other adventurer finds his way here and proclaims its presence to the world.'

'But the honours you deserve ... the fame,' she protested.

He silenced her protests with kisses. 'Ashes in the wind,' he said, and sweeping her up in his arms he began to run with her towards the creaming shallows.

9 781447 244769